D0260122

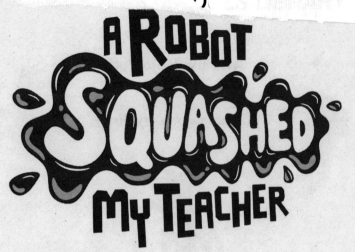

A ROBOT SQUASHED MY TEACHER

This book belongs to

_ _ _ _ _ _ _ _ _ _ _ _ _ _ _ _ _ _

Also by Pooja Puri

A Dinosaur Ate My Sister

POOJA PURI

A ROBOT SQUASHED MY TEACHER

Illustrated by
Allen Fatimaharan

MACMILLAN CHILDREN'S BOOKS

Published 2022 by Macmillan Children's Books
an imprint of Pan Macmillan
The Smithson, 6 Briset Street, London EC1M 5NR
EU representative: Macmillan Publishers Ireland Ltd,
1st Floor, The Liffey Trust Centre, 117-126 Sheriff Street Upper
Dublin 1, D01 YC43
Associated companies throughout the world
www.panmacmillan.com

ISBN 978-1-5290-7069-9

Text copyright © Pooja Puri 2022
Illustrations copyright © Allen Fatimaharan 2022

The right of Pooja Puri and Allen Fatimaharan to be identified as
the author and illustrator of this work has been asserted by them
in accordance with the Copyright, Designs and Patents Act 1988.

All rights reserved. No part of this publication may be reproduced,
stored in a retrieval system, or transmitted, in any form or by any means
(electronic, mechanical, photocopying, recording or otherwise),
without the prior written permission of the publisher.

Pan Macmillan does not have any control over, or any responsibility for,
any author or third-party websites referred to in or on this book.

1 3 5 7 9 8 6 4 2

A CIP catalogue record for this book is available from the British Library.

Printed and bound by CPI Group (UK) Ltd, Croydon CR0 4YY
Designed by Suzanne Cooper

COVENTRY EDUCATION &
LEARNING SERVICE

3 8002 02120 746 1		
Askews & Holts	30-Jun-2022	
JF P	£7.99	

This book   le or otherwise,
be lent, r   s prior consent
in any fo   . and without a
similar co   uent purchaser.

To all my teachers.
P.P.

Note From The Author

No ~~robots~~ teachers were harmed in the writing of this book.

Not really.

No authors were harmed in the writing of this book.

Not really

A Second Important Note From The Author

Before you start reading, there are a few things you should know:

1. I, Esha Verma, am a **genius inventor** extraordinaire.
2. I like lists.
3. I did not mean to turn my teacher into a pigeon. Some things just can't be helped.
4. Like all **genius inventors**, I have an apprentice. His name is **Broccoli**.
5. It is ~~my~~ our **dream of dreams** to win the Young Inventor of the Year contest.
6. If you've read my first **genius** journal, you will know this already.
7. If you have not read my first **genius** journal, I order you to stop being a DRONG, put down this book immediately and locate a copy. If you cannot find one in your nearest bookshop or library, I would have **VERY STERN WORDS** with the bookshop manager or the librarian.

This is the Brain Trophy.

⑧ Ready? Excellent. Then you will know that in our last adventure Broccoli and I travelled through time, were *almost* eaten by a T-rex, were actually eaten by a Guzzler and returned home without a time machine but with a dinosaur bone that turned out to be an egg.

⑨ Broccoli says that I have just given away a big **SPOILER**. I told him that I already warned you to read my first **genius** journal. If you hadn't read it yet, that is **YOUR OWN FAULT.**

A Letter from Secondus

TOOT TOOT, Esha, Broccoli and reptile,

Thank you for your letter and the *fifty* others before it. As I have already said *many times*, T.O.O.T. is very grateful for the Throat Ticklers you supplied, but they are definitely *not* looking for any new inventions at the moment.

I would also kindly remind you (again) that I am now a MOOT (Middle Officer of Time) and I am on a very important mission. Please *do not contact me* unless it is urgent. Situations classified as urgent are those that threaten all of time and space. They most definitely do NOT include: requiring a part for an invention, fixing an invention or anything else related to inventing.

TOOT TOOT,

Secondus Secondi

Another Letter from Secondus

No, I cannot tell you what the mission is because it is TOP SECRET.

No, I cannot take you on trips through time and space to help you find inspiration for genius inventions. That is against Section 55, Regulation 2.8 of Time Policies and Principles.

The Trouble with Being a <u>Genius Inventor</u>

The trouble with being a **genius inventor** is that you will always face obstacles in your quest for **genius-ness**. Obstacles like:

① DRONGS of sisters who steal your priceless inventions. (like time machines).

② Parents who cannot understand your **genius**. Take the Hole-in-the-floor Incident, for example. (If you haven't read my first **genius** journal, you won't know what I'm talking about and that's your own fault.)

When Mum and Dad saw it, their faces puffed up bigger than an exploding volcano.

I tried explaining to them that:

① The Hole-in-the-floor Incident was NOT my fault, but Nishi's.

② All **genius inventors** throughout history experienced setbacks.

(3) The cost of fixing the floor was really nothing in the Grand Scheme of Becoming a **Genius Inventor**.

Unfortunately, they did not see it the same way.

(Parents can be annoying like that.)

Instead they gave me an <u>**ULTIMATUM**</u>: 'Esha Verma, this is our final warning. One more inventing accident and you will not be allowed to enter the Young Inventor of the Year contest. You are skating on very thin ice. Do you understand?'

Albertus hatched a week later.

the dinosaur bone
that turned out
to be an egg →

How (Not) to
Train a T-rex

That was nine months ago.

In that time, Mum and Dad have grown extremely fond of Albertus. This is probably because they think he is a lizard. Nishi has tried telling them that he's a dinosaur, but fortunately they do not believe her. Unfortunately, training a T-rex is EXTREMELY difficult. Almost as difficult as winning the Brain Trophy. Absolutely more difficult than building a time machine.

For those of you who might be thinking about keeping a pet T-rex, you should know that there are no guides on caring for a dinosaur. Not a single one. Instead, you have to learn **ON THE JOB.**

[A note from Broccoli: A tortoise is far less trouble. A rabbit. Hamsters. Anything but a T-rex.]

During the last nine months, I have learnt seven important lessons about training a T-rex:

1. Toilet train your T-rex as soon as possible.
2. Do not leave any important objects near your T-rex.
3. They do not like loud noises (including Hoovers).
4. Do not say H-I-D-E or H-I-D-I-N-G in front of your T-rex. They will think you want to play hide-and-seek. (You will lose.)
5. Do not let them sleep on your bed.
6. They do not like baths. AT ALL.
7. They eat almost ANYTHING.

So far, Albertus has eaten exactly **SIX AND A HALF** of my **genius inventions**. After I found him chewing the third prototype of my Gecko Gloves, I decided that enough was enough. It was time for **SERIOUS ACTION.** And that, Reader, is how I came up with my **NEW genius invention.** That single, sparkling **BRAIN-ZINGER** that would win

me the Brain Trophy, get me inside the headquarters of Genius and Extraordinary Inventions Inc. (GENIE) and transform me into an

inventing legend FOREVER.

[A note from Broccoli: Or so we thought.]

The Brain-zinger

'Broccoli, I have it!' I announced as I sped into our classroom on Monday morning. He was hunched over his notebook at our corner table (specially selected by myself to hide our important conversations from nosey teachers and the less-genius members of my class). 'I finally have it!'

'So do I!' he said. He waved his notebook at me, which was covered in a complicated arrangement of formulae. 'I figured out what the Skunkles are missing.

NISHI'S WELLINGTON WHIFF!

It's the perfect nose-wrinkling ingredient. I've even calculated the concentration—'

'I'm not talking about the Skunkles,' I scoffed. 'I'm talking about a brain-zinger!'

'A brain-zinger?' He looked down at his notebook and sniffed. 'But I thought we were perfecting the Skunkles?'

'They can wait,' I said. '*This* cannot.' I waved my brand-new, latest-edition *Inventor's Handbook* at him (selling

Throat Ticklers to T.O.O.T. had proven excellent for my inventing funds). 'Do you remember Chapter 44? Brain-zingers can strike at any time and a **genius inventor** must ALWAYS be ready for when they do. This brain-zinger hit me at – well –' I realized I didn't know exactly, as Berty had **eaten** my alarm clock – 'this morning. I've been working on it since then.'

'Working on what?' said Broccoli suspiciously. He leaned back, his eyes fixed to my bag as if he were expecting something to explode or fly out of it.

[A note from Broccoli: That had actually happened before – twice.]

I cleared my throat, then stopped, suddenly remembering where I was.

Around me, the classroom was getting louder as everyone came in for morning registration. As always, Burper Bobby had a fizzy drink in his hand, Kevin and his gang were bouncing a football between them and the Two-plait Twins were arguing about their hair (yawn-boring-yawn).

'Stop worrying – Ernie's not here yet,' said Broccoli, sliding his notebook into his bag.

'You can never be too careful,' I said. 'Chapter 24 of the *Inventor's Handbook* says that a **genius inventor** must  be on guard for snoops and spies AT ALL TIMES. Have you forgotten what happened with the Camo-Conkers?' I sat down beside him and pulled out a roll of paper from my rucksack. 'Here it is,' I whispered, my fingers trembling with excitement as I handed it to my sniffly apprentice. 'This is the blueprint for the invention that is going to win us the Brain Trophy.'

Broccoli raised his eyebrows. 'That's what you said about the time machine.'

I snorted. 'It's not my fault they didn't read the note that we stuck on the dinosaur bone-egg. If they had, they would have realized it was **EVIDENCE** that we'd invented a working time machine. Anyway . . .' I cleared my throat. I did **NOT** want to be reminded about getting – shudder – last place. 'I know what you're thinking.'

'You do?' said Broccoli.

'How can we possibly invent something **better** than a time machine?'

'Actually, I wasn't—'

'Open it,' I said, pushing the blueprint towards him. 'Go on.'

Broccoli sniffed, picked it up extremely slowly, sniffed again, then he finally unfolded it. For a moment, he stared at it in silence.

'I knew it would stun you,' I said proudly. 'It's that genius.'

'I don't know if *stun* is the right word,' began Broccoli. He turned the blueprint upside-down, then back the right way. 'What does it do exactly?'

'What does it do?' We ducked as Kevin's football whizzed over our heads. 'Broccoli, this is the RoarEasy,' I said, lowering my voice so that only he could hear me. 'An invention that will let humans and animals TALK to each other. It was Berty who gave me the inspiration.'

'Albertus inspired you?' said Broccoli incredulously.

'Months it's taken me to train him! Months!'

'I'm not sure I'd call him trained,' said Broccoli. 'In fact, I still think we should ask Secondus to take him back to the Cretaceous—'

'We're only halfway there,' I interrupted, pretending not to hear him. (As I had already told Broccoli, I was not sending Berty back to the Age of the Dinosaurs. It was far too dangerous for him. And who would teach him about the brilliance of inventing?)

'He's still got so much to learn,' I continued. 'Imagine how much easier it would be if we could understand each other?' I jabbed the blueprint. 'That's where the RoarEasy comes in. An all-in-one translation device for humans and animals.'

'I don't know,' said Broccoli, chewing his lip. His snot wobbled as he examined the blueprint again. 'This seems . . . difficult. And potentially dangerous. Like the time machine.'

'But that's why it's so **GENIUS**,' I said. 'Safe and simple inventions are never going to win the Brain Trophy. You have to think outside the box. In fact, you have to invent a new box.'

Broccoli blinked. 'A new box?'

'Precisely,' I said. 'Just like we did with the Throat Tickler. I have a special

SPINGLY-TINGLY feeling

...ut this one, Broccoli. I can feel it in my fingers and toes. Can't you?'

He hesitated. 'Well, I wouldn't say—'

'And Chapter 59 of the *Inventor's Handbook* says that you should always listen to spingly feelings, remember? Come on – you'd even be able to talk to Archibald,' I added slyly.

(I have, in fact, understood Archibald ever since he was delivered to Broccoli. That is because he is not a normal animal and is, in fact, an

EVIL ALIEN BEING disguised as a tortoise.

For some reason, nobody except me is able to see it.)

[A note from Broccoli: Very funny, Esha.]

Broccoli's face brightened in sudden realization. 'Talk to Archie?' he said, his snot jiggling with MEGA excitement. 'You really think I could? I've tried so many times: I've asked Granny Bertha, I've borrowed books about tortoise communication from the library, but nothing seems to work—'

'Think about it, Broccoli,' I said. 'If we have devices that can translate different languages, we can absolutely translate animal speak for humans and human speak for animals. You and Archibald would be able to have **REAL CONVERSATIONS.**'

'Real conversations,' murmured Broccoli, staring dreamily into space.

[A note from Broccoli: I did not do this.]

He inspected the blueprint again for a long minute. 'I *suppose* it can't really be as difficult or as dangerous as inventing a time machine,' he said slowly.

'And,' I reminded him, 'if we can escape a Guzzler, we can absolutely invent a translation device.'

'Just imagine what Granny Bertha will say if we invent a machine that can talk to tortoises,' said Broccoli. He beamed. 'She'll never believe it! And Archibald will be delighted!'

'This isn't just an invention,' I declared. 'It's a moment of **REVOLUTIONARY CHANGE.** This will win us the Young Inventor of the Year contest.'

'Hello, **WORMS,**' said a shrill voice. A scrawny hand clapped down on the desk. I looked up to find Ernie Rathbone, AKA my **ARCH-NEMESIS**, sneering over us. 'Did I hear someone mention the Young Inventor of the Year contest?'

A brief but important interruption about Ernie Rathbone AKA my arch-nemesis

ERNIE RATHBONE

EMPTY AIR FOR BRAINS

ARCH NEMESIS

What you need to know: ←

1. Ernie Rathbone joined our school a few months ago. Since then, we have become SWORN ENEMIES of the Tesla–Edison kind.

2. Ernie thinks he is a **genius inventor**. He is NOT.

3. He thinks that he is a better inventor than me. He is an **AIR-BRAIN**.

4. Like me, he wants to win the Brain Trophy. Unlike me, he has a **BELOW ZERO** chance of succeeding.

5. His uncle, Professor Rathbone, is Head of Research at the Central Research Laboratory, which has some of the **COOLEST** experiments in the entire country. I have wanted to visit **FOREVER**. Unfortunately, it hardly ever opens to visitors. Even more unfortunately, Ernie is allowed to visit whenever he wants (I know this because he has told me a **GAZILLION** times).

'That's none of your business, Rat-Bone,' I hissed.

'You won't be saying that when I win the contest,' he smirked. 'I don't know where I'll put the Brain Trophy when I win it. I've got so many prizes already.' His smirk widened. 'But that's to be expected when you're a **genius** like me.'

I snorted loudly. 'If you're so **genius**, why were you snooping around in my bag last week?'

'Esha,' said Broccoli with a warning sniff.

(OK, so maybe I should have just ignored Ernie, but he really was the most pestilent pustule I had ever met.)

Ernie flushed. 'I wasn't snooping. I was *investigating*. Chapter 45 of the *Inventor's Handbook* says that the best **inventors** always have an ear and eye open for—'

'We know what the *Inventor's Handbook* says, Rat-Bone,' I growled.

'And what's this?' His eye fell on my top-secret blueprint. 'The first prototype of the Roar—'

'Like I said,' I snapped, snatching it away from him before he could read any more, '**NONE OF YOUR BUSINESS.**'

Unfortunately, Ernie already had his fingers on it.

'Let go, Rat-Bone!' I shouted.

'Why don't you make me?'

Broccoli (unhelpfully) sneezed and glanced at the door. 'Esha, Monsieur Crépeau will be here any mom—'

'Do you really think you have a chance of beating me,

Verma?' interrupted Ernie. 'My uncle is Head of Research at the **Central Research Laboratory**. He won the Brain Trophy when he was just ten years old *and* he's been a judge. **Genius** runs in our family. You're just a

silly. Little. **GIRL.**

A **bubble** of anger burst inside me. 'I said . . . let GO!' I snapped, tugging the blueprint so hard that Ernie lost his balance and tumbled forward, almost falling flat on to the table.

 **'ESHA VERMA.'**

The voice of our class tutor, Monsieur Crépeau, boomed across the classroom like a foghorn.
UH-OH.

A thing or ~~two~~ four to know about Monsieur Crépeau:

① When he was younger, he appeared on TV for three minutes. He has wanted to be a TV star ever since. (This is important to know for later.)

② He teaches us French. (Monsieur Crépeau says this is just a SHORT-TERM plan. Turns out that becoming a TV star takes time.)

③ He thinks I am trouble with a capital T.

④ His *ears* are like **HUGE** satellites. This means they are always ready to plug into someone else's business.

'What are you doing?' said Monsieur Crépeau. His moustache, which stuck out on either side of his face like a pair of bristly feathers, quivered dangerously.

Broccoli sneezed.

The Two-plait Twins giggled.

Ernie straightened up and pointed a finger at me.

'She started it, Monsieur Crépeau,' he whined.

'He's lying!' I snapped. 'He was trying to steal my blueprint for the Young Inventor of the Year cont—'

'Not that again,' said Monsieur Crépeau wearily.

(Another thing to know about Monsieur Crépeau: he does not understand the magic of inventing. This is because his brain is already stuffed with French nouns and TV.)

'Ernie, to your seat. Esha, your *inventions* have already got you five detentions this term.' His words SHIMMIED across the air like angry fireflies. 'One more and I will be speaking to your parents.'

'I didn't do anything,' I protested. 'Ernie was the one who—'

'And I don't want to hear another word about that ridiculous contest,' he continued.

'But—'

'Do you understand?' said Monsieur Crépeau again, his eyes **bulging** at me.

I swallowed.

Mum and Dad had already given me a FINAL WARNING. No way would they let me enter the Young Inventor of the Year contest if Monsieur Crépeau told them about the detentions (which, by the way, were all Ernie's fault. I'd tried telling Monsieur Crépeau, but he would not listen. That's teachers for you). 'Yes, Mr Crépeau.'

'Monsieur.' He sighed. 'Everyone, please get your books out.'

'I don't think he's forgiven you for the time you turned his eyebrows purple,' whispered Broccoli.

'That was supposed to happen to Ernie! It's not my fault he walked past his table at the wrong moment. Anyway, he never properly found out who was responsible for that – he only *suspects* it's me.'

'Either way,' said Broccoli, 'Ernie's trouble. Don't you remember what happened with the Rotten Egg-ploder? I told you not to leave that in his rucksack.' He sniffed. 'The classroom still stinks *and* we got a detention.'

'That was payback for his Gluey Chewies. Took hours for my teeth to unstick. Besides, it was worth it to see the look on his face. Totally PONGWHIFFED.'

Ernie turned round and sneered in my direction. I made a note to myself to invent a pair of vaporizing glasses at the earliest opportunity.

'We can't let him win the Brain Trophy, Broccoli.' I slid the blueprint into my bag. 'It's only six weeks until the contest. That means we have to start inventing the RoarEasy immediately.'

Building the RoarEasy: the Top-secret Method

If you've read my first journal, you will know that a **genius inventor** NEVER reveals their secrets. If you were hoping things would be different this time, you are an **AIR-BRAIN**.

~~[A note from Broccoli: Building a RoarEasy is even more difficult and far more dangerous than I'd expected. I have convinced Esha to include a timeline to help you understand why you should definitely not try to build one at home.]~~

SIX WEEKS BEFORE THE CONTEST

FIVE WEEKS BEFORE THE CONTEST

THREE WEEKS BEFORE THE CONTEST

ONE WEEK BEFORE THE CONTEST...

The Friday Our Plans
Went ~~Pear~~ Pigeon-shaped

Thinking about it, I should've known that things were going to turn out **pigeon-shaped** when my alarm didn't go off on Friday morning. (Albertus had eaten my back-up clock.) He had ALSO **gobbled** through my Inventor's Safe and started nibbling the ready-for-trialling-and-testing RoarEasy. By the time I was able to wrestle it off him, I was LATE for school. By the time I got a good look at the RoarEasy, I knew we had a PROBLEM. Fortunately, Monsieur Crépeau still wasn't in the classroom when I arrived.

'What do you think, Verma?' asked Ernie, whizzing past me on his jet-powered skateboard with a grin. 'Double turbines. Eco boost. Quick or what?'

'For the HUNDREDTH time, Rat-Bone,' I hissed, 'I DON'T CARE about your stupid skateboard.'

'It's brilliant, Ernie,' said the Two-plait Twins together.

'This is nothing,' he boasted. 'You should see some of the experiments my uncle has at the Central Research Laboratory.'

'What kind of experiments?' said the Two-plait Twins.

He dropped his voice to a whisper and tapped his nose knowingly.

'Top-secret ones.'

Oh, please.

'You can normally only see them if you work there, but this year my uncle's giving away twenty exclusive tickets in a **special raffle**. Only the luckiest will get a chance to see the laboratory.' He smirked. 'But *I'm* allowed inside whenever I want.'

(OK, so maybe I was a teensy-tiny bit curious about the raffle, but I would rather eat a smelly sock than ask Ernie.)

'Bet you're not even allowed to see the experiments,' I snorted.

'Am too,' retorted Ernie. 'In fact, I'm going to be my uncle's protégé.'

'Potty – what?'

The Two-plait Twins giggled.

'Protégé,' said Ernie with a scowl. 'As soon as I win the Young Inventor of the Year contest and prove that I'm ready to work with him, *I'm* going to help him take the laboratory to a whole new level of **genius**. He's even given me a workshop.'

'A workshop?' I scoffed. 'Unlike you, Rat-Bone, I don't need a workshop for inventing. My **genius** brain is enough. And if you think your skateboard is going to win you the Brain Trophy you're an **AIR-BRAIN**.'

'This?' Ernie sniggered. 'Don't be silly, Verma. This was just a little something I put together for fun. My invention for the contest is something **spectacular**.'

He circled past me in a puff of green smoke, zoomed through the tables, then wheeled round Broccoli, who had just entered the classroom. 'If I were you, I wouldn't even bother entering the contest. In two days, I'm going to be crowned the **Young Inventor of the Year**. There's no way you and your apprentice are going to BEAT me.'

I scowled as he skated away, thinking of the CHEWED RoarEasy in my rucksack.

'Do you want the *bad* news or the EVEN **MORE TERRIBLE** news?' I huffed as Broccoli slid in next to me.

He sniffed.

'I'll start with the bad,' I continued.

'It's just awful,' whispered Broccoli.

'You don't need to remind me,' I said, unzipping my rucksack so I could show him the RoarEasy's newly BOTCHED wiring.

'Awful,' echoed Broccoli again.

Thank goodness he understood the DREADFULNESS of our situation.

'That's why I brought it with me. I can't be listening to YAWN-BORING teachers when we have a **genius invention** to get ready for—'

'They might take Archibald away,' murmured Broccoli.

[An apology from Broccoli: Dear Reader, I am sorry about this page. Just the thought of Archie being taken away from me sent me into a sneezing fit.]

'What?'

'Archibald,' echoed Broccoli. He pulled an **OFFICIAL-LOOKING** letter out of his pocket and handed it to me, his face pale. 'Read it.'

I clicked my tongue with impatience and unfolded the letter (which was crusty with snot).

Dear James Bertha Darwin,

It has come to our attention that you are the rare and lucky owner of a tortoise. As part of our mission to ensure the health and happiness of tortoises everywhere, we will be carrying out an inspection of your beloved pet on 15 June.

To pass this inspection, your tortoise must qualify as a happy and healthy tortoise. A checklist with further details has been included.

If your care of the tortoise is found to be unsatisfactory in any way, your tortoise will be rehomed elsewhere. If you refuse to co-operate with us, your details will be passed on to the relevant authorities for appropriate action.

We look forward to seeing you and your tortoise on 15 June.

Yours,

Shelbus Sheldon

President of the Tortoise Welfare Society

(T.W.S.)

'Isn't it just awful?' sniffed Broccoli. 'Granny Bertha's warned me about the T.W.S. They're strict. *Super* strict.' He dabbed his nose woefully. 'They almost took Archimedes away because his shell didn't have enough shine.'

'*Bonjour*, everyone,' said Monsieur Crépeau, waddling into the classroom. 'What an excellent morning it is! Ernie, get off that skateboard and sit down. Could someone please open the window? I can still smell rotten eggs.'

'Awful?' I snapped impatiently. 'Broccoli, have you been listening to me? Albertus has **BOTCHED** all the wiring in the RoarEasy! **It's a <u>disaster</u>.**'

[A note from Broccoli: I did warn Esha that the Inventor's Safe wouldn't keep out a T-rex.]

(The Inventor's Safe is, in fact, supposed to keep out prying parents, snooping sisters and ravenous reptiles. I have now written to the manufacturer to demand my money back.)

'This –' I waved the letter at him – '*this* is nothing to be worrying about!'

'Nothing to worry about?' echoed Broccoli. His snot trembled with indignation, his voice a **HOARSE** squeak. 'The inspection is only TWO days away!'

'I have a special announcement,' said Monsieur Crépeau.

'So is the contest!' I snapped. Honestly, it was like Broccoli had forgotten that we were trying to win the Brain Trophy. 'That's why I brought the RoarEasy with me—'

'– unsatisfactory in any way—' murmured Broccoli, re-reading the letter.

'Broccoli, will you stop flapping and listen to—'

'I know that most of you will have heard about the Young Inventor of the Year contest,' continued Monsieur Crépeau.

My head shot up at once, my inventor's instincts suddenly on **RED ALERT**. For the first time **EVER**, Monsieur Crépeau was actually *smiling*.

'An – ah – exciting competition to find – ah – the best young inventor. As always, **Genius and Extraordinary Inventions Inc.** has randomly selected ten guest judges from across the country to help them make their decision.'

My inventor's instincts were now even (pricklier) than a cactus.

Burper Bobby was picking his nose. The Two-plait Twins were yawning. The only other person who seemed to be

paying any attention was Ernie, who was leaning so far forward that he was almost hovering above his chair.

Monsieur Crépeau's moustache twitched as he looked around the classroom.

Then . . .

(Take a breath, Reader.)

'I am honoured to tell you that I will be one of the guest judges,' he declared.

My mouth dropped.

It couldn't be true. *Monsieur Crépeau?* He didn't even *like* inventing.

'GENIE is keen to have judges with a range of experience and knowledge, such as myself—'

I snorted.

Monsieur Crépeau was looking into the distance as he spoke. 'Finally, I, Monsieur Crépeau, teacher of French, luminary of young minds, will have the chance to star on TV again.' He beamed. 'It will make me – and, of course, our school – Boffington Academy – famous throughout the country—'

(Told you it was important.)

'Can you believe this?' I whispered to Broccoli.

My sniffly apprentice was still staring at the letter.

I rolled my eyes.

(OBVIOUSLY, chewed inventions are far more IMPORTANT than tortoise inspections.)

[A note from Broccoli: That is a matter of opinion.]

'Bribery, blackmail, implosion, transformation, diffusion, etc. of a guest judge is strictly against the rules and will result in instant disqualification.'

EURGH.

This was turning out to be the worst Friday of my **ENTIRE LIFE.**

And it was about to get

 even **WORSE** . . .

Broccoli has interrupted to point out that we wouldn't have got the Detention of Doom if I hadn't tried to stick that banana skin into Ernie's skateboard turbine. I have reminded him that it was Ernie's own fault for trying to snoop in my bag (AGAIN). It was also not my fault that Monsieur Crépeau walked in at that exact moment.

[A note from Broccoli: I did tell Esha that the banana skin was a bad idea, but, as usual, she did not listen.]

The Detention of Doom

I glanced impatiently at the clock. 'This is a waste of time,' I whispered to Broccoli, who had already filled up a page of his book. 'If we don't have the RoarEasy ready before the contest, we're going to be **HUMILIATED**. Ernie will never let us hear the end of it.'

'The quicker we finish copying these nouns, the quicker we can leave,' said Broccoli, his pen whizzing across the paper.

'Silence,' said Monsieur Crépeau without looking up.

I scowled. With one eye on Monsieur Crépeau, I slid the RoarEasy out of my rucksack and on to my lap, making sure it was hidden behind the desk.

'You're going to get us in trouble,' whispered Broccoli.

'We're in trouble already,' I pointed out.

'I don't think you should be fiddling with it here,' began Broccoli. 'Don't you remember what happened when the voice synthesizer flew out of the control panel? It almost *set fire* to Mum's tomatoes.' He sniffed. 'You should wait until we get home.'

I ignored him and clicked open the control panel (or what was left of it).

Suddenly there was a **loud** flapping noise above us. I looked up to find a pigeon hovering in the air, its bird eyes blinking down at us with curiosity.

'Not again,' muttered Monsieur Crépeau, jumping to his feet. 'I knew I should have closed that window. Go on – out – SHOO!' The pigeon made a startled noise and flapped towards the ceiling, out of reach.

Monsieur Crépeau waved his arms at the bird. 'Repulsive vermin. James, shut the door so it doesn't escape!'

'Yes, Monsieur Crépeau,' said Broccoli, darting to his feet.

I rolled my eyes and looked down at the RoarEasy. Using my special inventor's tweezers, I tugged the blue wire back into position – at least, that's what I was trying to do.

Unfortunately, the pigeon decided to dive towards me at that particular moment.

Even more unfortunately, my hand slipped, pulling the blue wire completely out of the RoarEasy.

It made a **long**, SHRILL whistling
noise like a kettle and hopped upwards.

'Esha?' squeaked Broccoli.

The RoarEasy **LEAPT** across my desk
like a turbo-powered frog and

flew into the air.

It bounced and spun. It danced across the classroom so
ferociously that it looked as if it were about to launch
itself into outer space.

With a frightened warble, the pigeon flapped away in
the opposite direction.

'Esha Verma!' said Monsieur Crépeau. 'This is no time for—'

That's when something peculiar happened.

Before I could move, the RoarEasy ejected a bolt of
fizzing blue sparks at Monsieur Crépeau.

PHITIZZZZZZZZZ!

Monsieur Crépeau hopped and jiggled just
like the RoarEasy, his moustache fluttering
like the sails of a ship.

'ESHA-A-A-A-A!' he cried as he shot into the air like a rocket. He twisted round, his entire body

PHITIZZZZZZZING

with

blue sparks.

My jaw dropped.

'We have to do something!' squealed Broccoli, his snot dangling to **WILD WOBBLE** mode.

A cloud of yellow smoke puffed out of the RoarEasy, blocking Monsieur Crépeau from view.

The air *whooshed* around us.

I felt myself being lifted upwards. Broccoli grabbed a table, shrieking as he began to rise off the floor. The pigeon warbled, flapping furiously against the wind. A few feathers fluttered off its wings and spiralled into the storm of blue sparks. With a disgruntled warble, it pulled itself clear and disappeared out through a window.

There was another **PHITIZZZZING** of sparks.

The lights flashed on and off. The windows **rattled**.

'WH-AT'S HAPPE-N-ING?' gasped Broccoli.

Then, as suddenly as it had started, everything stopped.

The lights flickered on.

The windows fell still.

With a loud rush of air, the smoke spiralled back into the RoarEasy and disappeared.

The desk fell down with a bump.

I looked at my shoes and noted, with some disappointment, that I was back on the ground.

Broccoli was shaking from head to toe, his fingers clamped round the table. His hair was standing up as if he'd been *electrocuted*, the orange ends still twitching with fright.

'Monsieur Crépeau?' I said.

But there was no sign of him. Well, almost no sign, because, as I stepped forward, I saw his clothes on the desk. A few blue sparks flashed around his jumper then vanished. UH-OH.

I picked up the RoarEasy, which had fallen on the floor. A single charred pigeon feather was stuck between the wires.

'Wh-where is he?' Broccoli whimpered. He looked at the clothes, his face turning paler than curdled custard.

He took a step back. 'I don't believe it,' he squeaked.

'I think – I think we made him

disappear.

That's when the clothes moved.

We jumped back.

'Did you see that?' shrieked Broccoli.

'Course I saw it,' I hissed.

The clothes moved again.

Broccoli took another step back.

Fortunately, I'd had a lot of practice dealing with

DINOSAURS so I was **not** scared. Not one bit. Instead,

I grabbed a book from the desk and held it over my head.

A small round bump was **wriggling** its way up through the

folds. I licked my lips, ready to splat whatever might . . .

Suddenly, a feathered head popped out of Monsieur

Crépeau's shirt.

I breathed in sharply. 'Is that—'

'A pigeon,' finished Broccoli.

The pigeon blinked at us. It was silvery

grey with turquoise feathers. But what

was peculiar – besides the fact that it had

emerged from Monsieur Crépeau's clothes – was that it had two feathers spiralling out on either side of its beak, almost like a . . .

Wait just a moment.

'I thought it flew out the window,' said Broccoli in puzzlement.

'It did.' I stared more closely at the bird. It glared back at me with a familiar grumpy expression.

A wave of

ICE-COLD realization

passed over me.

The pigeon stepped forward, then stopped suddenly, its eyes widening as it glanced at its feet.

'Monsieur Crépeau?' I stepped towards the bird. 'Is that *you?*'

'What are you talking about?' squeaked Broccoli. 'That's a pigeon!'

The pigeon opened its beak and –

'SQUAWK!'

The noise was so **loud** and unexpected that it stumbled back in surprise. Wobbling across the desk, it tried to grab a pen, which rolled on to the carpet. With another wild SQUAWK, it jabbed at the exercise books with its beak: MONSIEUR CRÉPEAU. Then it blinked at me.

I grinned. 'Monsieur Crépeau! I knew it was you!'

Monsieur Crépeau's head bobbed back in outrage. 'SQUAWK – SQUAWK,' he said, as if to say, 'what are *you* looking so happy about?'.

Broccoli looked the pigeon up and down, his mouth frozen somewhere between shock and confusion. 'But – how – I don't understand. Pigeons don't squawk.'

Honestly.

'Teachers don't turn into pigeons either,' I said. 'What we're dealing with here is extremely unusual.'

Monsieur Crépeau warbled in agreement.

'What are we going to do?' whispered Broccoli. 'We can't leave him here!'

I stared at Monsieur Crépeau, my brain whirring at TOP SPEED. He must have guessed what I was thinking. Spinning round, he started waddling across the table.

'No, you don't,' I said, leaping forward. His eyes widened as he glanced back. With a wild squawk, he drew out his wings and . . . fell flat on to the desk. His pigeon feet cycled helplessly in the air as I shoved him into my rucksack.

'What are you doing?' said Broccoli in horror. 'That's kidnap!'

'Birdnap, actually,' I pointed out. 'And we don't have any other choice. Do you want to be disqualified from the contest? Grab his clothes. I'm not losing the Brain Trophy to Rat-Bone because of a slight malfunction. This calls for an urgent and serious INVESTIGATION.'

An Urgent and
Serious Investigation

We cycled home at *lightning speed*,
collected Archibald, snuck past Mum
and Dad, who were, thankfully,
hanging a new washing-line in the garden (Berty had eaten
the old one), and dived into my room. Only when we were
safely inside did I open my rucksack.

   'Monsieur Crépeau?' I said. 'You can come out now.'

   He wobbled dizzily onto the carpet. His feathers
were **sticking up** all over the place and his legs were
trembling.

   Archibald was staring at Monsieur Crépeau as if he
were the most interesting thing **he'd ever seen**. He
plodded closer, sniffed him and began

HALOOTING

with laughter.

Monsieur Crépeau looked at his feathery legs, then he began stomping across the carpet. His head bobbed sideways as he

SQUAWKED

at us. The squawks were sharp and unmistakeably **ANGRY**.

'I'm sorry, Monsieur Crépeau, but would you mind being quieter?' I interrupted quickly. 'I can't let my parents or my DRON— sister find out about you.'

Monsieur Crépeau glared at me and made a **rude noise** at the back of his throat.

'Besides, we don't know what you're saying. You're speaking bird – well, pigeon – well, we're not quite sure what it is, actually. On the bright side, you can understand us.' I grinned. 'That means the RoarEasy *almost* works.'

Monsieur Crépeau's left eyelid flickered.

'What are we going to do?' whispered Broccoli. 'If Mrs Pickles finds out the truth, we'll be expelled.' He looked **queasier** than a rotten egg. 'Mum and Dad will be so disappointed! And what if the T.W.S. hear about it?'

He sniffed, his snot trembling. 'I told you

NOT to fiddle

with the RoarEasy.

Now look what's happened!'

'It's not MY fault that pigeon flew in at that exact moment, is it?' I snapped. 'That was just *bad timing*.'

He pulled out the inspection letter and waved it in the air. 'A tortoise owner should be kind, trustworthy and *responsible* – that's what it says on their checklist! If they find out we turned our teacher into a pigeon, they'll definitely take Archibald away!'

'Broccoli—'

'I was supposed to start preparing him for the inspection toni— OW!'

Broccoli rubbed his arm where I'd pinched him.

'Will you stop babbling and listen?' I snapped. 'Nobody is being expelled. And there is absolutely no way that either of our parents, the Tortoise Welfare Society or GENIE are going to find out about this. We're going to **FIX IT**, OK?'

TORTOISE WELFARE SOCIETY

Broccoli sniffed, his eyes wet and watery. 'We are?'

'Course we are,' I snorted. 'We've travelled through all of the Murkle, remember? We've fought **wormhole worms**, escaped a **T-rex** and a *Guzzler*. **This'll be easy.'** I bent down and looked Monsieur Crépeau seriously in the eye. 'I'm sorry about turning you into a pigeon, Monsieur Crépeau, but it's only a slight – uh – hiccup.'

Monsieur Crépeau eyeballed me in disgust.

'Luckily for you, I'm a **genius inventor** and Broccoli is my apprentice. If there is *anyone* who can turn you back into a human, it's us. That means we're all going to have to work together. In return, I'd appreciate it if you wouldn't mention this – uh – **pigeon event** to anyone. In fact, it probably would be better if you forgot it ever happened. What do you say?'

I held out my hand.

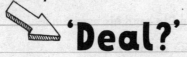 **'Deal?'**

Monsieur Crépeau was staring at me as if he would rather be thrown into a pigeon pie.

'Unless you'd rather stay a pigeon?'

Warbling unhappily, he touched his beak against the tip of my finger.

I grinned. 'That wasn't so hard, was it?' Darting to my bookshelf, I pulled out everything I'd gathered on translation devices. 'We can figure this out. It won't take long.'

Exactly thirty-three minutes and twenty-seven seconds later, I found what I was looking for. (I am quite sure that this must be a record time for **urgent** and **serious investigations.** Take that, Thomas Edison.)

'Here it is!' I cried, leaping up in excitement. The pile of books beside me toppled over, narrowly missing Monsieur Crépeau, who squawked in annoyance.

Broccoli looked up from Mum's laptop.

Archibald continued to read his magazine (*The Ultimate Tortoise Getaway*).

'It's in here.' I waved a book at Broccoli. '*Human-animal Translation Devices: A History of Malfunctions.*' I cleared my throat. 'Although a human-animal translation device is yet to be successfully invented, there have been plenty of **inventors** who have tried. Anyone planning to create such a device should **beware** the Transmogrify Malfunction.'

Broccoli frowned. 'Didn't you tell me you'd read that book—'

'This particular malfunction is known to transform humans into animals,' I continued loudly. (Honestly, how is a **genius inventor** meant to read everything? That is a job for *apprentices*.)

[A note from Broccoli: I'm quite sure that's not in the Apprentice-Inventor Agreement.]

'The cause is still unknown. Fortunately, research has shown that the process can be REVERSED with a **molecular modulator**. Once installed to your

53

device, the molecular modulator will generate an *INVERSE* effect, which will **undo** the transformation.' I grinned at Broccoli.

'That's what **WE** need!
A molecular modulator!'

'Where do we find one of those?'

'I – uh – it doesn't say,' I said in disappointment, scanning the pages. 'But it does say that it would take us months of work to create one ourselves, so we don't have enough time to invent one.'

'ESHA!' Nishi's voice suddenly EXPLODED from outside.

Archibald looked up with a delighted grin.

'Quick – under the bed!' I hissed at Monsieur Crépeau. He blinked at me in disgust. 'Go on!'

With a slow shuffle, he waddled towards it and hid himself from view. A second later, Nishi marched into my room, holding Albertus under her arm. Out of the corner of my eye, I saw Broccoli typing furiously on Mum's laptop.

'Look what your T-rex almost did!' Nishi brandished a pair of golden tickets at me.

54

'He **ALMOST ATE** my

WINNING

⬆ TICKETS.

Luckily, I saved them in time.'

Albertus burbled and looked down at his feet.

'It's not his fault,' I said. 'He was probably hungry.'

'Hungry? Do you even know what these are?'

'I'm sure you're about to tell us.'

'These are a pair of tickets to the **Central Research Laboratory**,' she said, fanning them in the air. 'I won them in their special raffle. They came through the post today.'

(I know what you're thinking. How did my DRONG of a sister win tickets to the Central Research Laboratory? Sometimes, life is just so **UNFAIR**.)

I **stared** at her. 'The Central Research Laboratory?' I said. 'You didn't even tell me you'd entered a raffle—'

'I did too,' said Nishi. 'It's not my fault that you don't listen to anyone but yourself.'

I folded my arms across my chest. 'That's not true.'

[A note from Broccoli: Well . . .]

'They're sending a limousine to collect me and Mum. We'll get an exclusive tour behind the laboratory's weather experiments AND see the grand opening of the Weather Simulation Room. They're even inviting a TV crew from SCIENCE TODAY to film it. All the raffle winners are going to be interviewed.' She plonked Berty into my arms. 'It'll be my first interview as a GUM meteorologist so keep *him* away from my room. I have to prepare.' She spun on her heel and marched out of the room.

'This could launch me into *meteorological STARDOM . . .*'

The door slammed shut behind her.

Albertus burbled softly.

'Tell me about it,' I said.

Monsieur Crépeau wobbled out, his eyes quivering as he caught sight of Albertus.

'Monsieur Crépeau, meet Albertus, my pet – ah –

lizard,' I said. Somehow, I didn't think it was a good idea to tell him about Albertus being a **T-rex**.

'Esha, I've got it,' said Broccoli. He pointed at the laptop. 'It says here that there are three molecular modulators in existence. One is in India, one in America and the third in Brazil.'

My heart dropped to my toes.

The plan for changing Monsieur Crépeau back to human form had suddenly gone from **VERY DIFFICULT** to

ULTRA

IMPOSSIBLE.

'No, wait,' said Broccoli. His eyes moved across the screen. 'India have loaned their molecular modulator to England for three months. It's being kept at –' He breathed in sharply and leaned so close to the laptop that his snot almost touched the keyboard. 'I don't believe it.'

'WHERE?' I said sharply.

'At the Central Research Laboratory.'

I **GOGGLED** at him, my inventor's instincts
sparkling with SPINGLY-TINGLY delight.

Archibald's eyes widened as if to say, 'you've got to be
joking'.

I grinned at Broccoli.

'No,' he said, shaking his head. 'We're not doing that.'

Monsieur Crépeau warbled, his head swivelling worriedly
between us.

'I haven't even told you my **genius** idea yet.'

'We're **not** breaking into the Central Research
Laboratory and we're **definitely not** stealing the
molecular modulator,' said Broccoli.

'Course we're not,' I snorted incredulously. 'We're not
breaking into the Central Research Laboratory because
we're going to use Nishi's tickets. And we're not going to
steal the molecular modulator. We're going to **BORROW**
it. And I know exactly how . . .'

~~How to Trick a DRONG~~
The Master Plan

I am sure that you, the Reader, are foot-hoppingly desperate to know my **GENIUS** master plan of getting us inside the Central Research Laboratory, so I have included a checklist of our Four-step Method below:

~~[A note from Broccoli: I would like to remind you, the Reader, that laboratories are dangerous places and I would not advise anyone to enter one without adult supervision.]~~

STEP ONE: GET NISHI'S TICKETS
METHOD: THE ALBERTUS

STEP FOUR : THE DECOY
METHOD : MAKE A SECRET PHONE CALL (MORE ABOUT THAT LATER)

LIMOS ARE US

'Your limousine's here!' I shouted.

'Already?' shrieked Nishi. 'But it's ten minutes early!'

'If you're not ready, I can go instead,' I said sweetly.

She gave me an EVIL look, checked her hair in the

mirror (for the HUNDREDTH time) and ran to the door.

'You wish! **Hurry up, Mum!**'

A moment later, Mum charged out of the kitchen, her

ear fixed to her phone. 'Yes, Aunty Usha — Nishi, have you

got the tickets? — Esha, keep an eye on Albertus,

please—'

'Yes, Mum,' I said, giving her my best

ANGEL FACE.

'Come on, Mum!' Nishi was already out of the door. 'I can't miss the start of the tour!' She was so excited that, for one teensy-tiny moment, I almost felt guilty about my **GENIUS** plan. 'Shame you won't get to see the laboratory!' she continued, smirking back at me. 'You'll have to watch *me* on **TV** instead. Just like all the **LOSERS** who didn't win tickets!'

All my guilt popped in an instant. What my DRONG of a sister didn't know was that the tickets in her bag were, in fact,

VERY CLEVER

→ **DUPLICATES.**
DUPLICATES.

The **real** tickets were actually in my pocket. What she *also* didn't know was that the limousine outside was

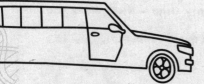 NOT the limousine sent by the Central Research Laboratory. It was, in

fact, a **DECOY** arranged by my **genius** self (with my Throat Tickler money, of course).

I grinned. 'Hope you don't freeze on camera, DRONG-BRAIN.'

'We'll get you something from the gift shop, love,' called Mum as she entered the limousine after Nishi. I waited until they had disappeared round the corner, then I charged up to my room.

'That's Stage One of Mission Molecular Modulator complete,' I said to Monsieur Crépeau, who was perched on the windowsill.

His beady eye quivered at me in disapproval.

'Next – the **INVENTORY.**'

INVENTORY

Monsieur Crépeau flapped his wings impatiently.

'A **genius inventor** must *always* carry out an inventory before an important mission,' I said, peering at the list. 'RoarEasy – check.'

Monsieur Crépeau glared at it.

'Nishi's tickets – check,' I continued, pretending not to notice. 'Skunkles – check. Go-Glider – check. Earscope – check.' Monsieur Crépeau squawked at me. 'Expanding Gumdrops – check.' Waddling across my bed, he picked up a pencil in his beak and *scratched* it across the notebook I'd given him for communicating. 'C – A – what's that?' I said, squinting at the page. 'R – no – N – M – that looks nothing like an M – E – R – oh – *cameras?* Do you mean security cameras?' Monsieur Crépeau nodded. 'You don't have to worry your feathery head about those. The Pow-Punch – check. I remember Ernie telling us that his uncle doesn't use them in the laboratory. Gecko Gloves – check. Slimer Shot. Thinks they're too easy to hack. Inventor's Torch. Check – check. Your duplicate ticket for when we change you back. Check.' I pulled out a small blue band from my drawer. 'Pet tracker – check.'

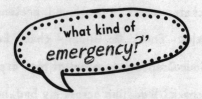

Monsieur Crépeau's feathery moustache wobbled as he bobbed his head in an unmistakeable **'no'**.

I sighed. 'I've told you, Monsieur Crépeau. It's only to keep track of you in case of an emergency.'

'SQUAWK!' he said, as if to say,

'what kind of emergency?'

'I don't know. That's why it's an emergency. You won't even know it's there.' I looked at him sternly. 'It's for your own protection.'

Monsieur Crépeau rolled his eyes, then stuck his foot out towards me.

'Thank you,' I said, gently clipping the band over his leg. I held the rucksack out to him. 'Now, if you could please get inside.'

'SQUAWK-SQUAWK!' screeched Monsieur Crépeau, the feathers on his neck puffing up in outrage.

'You can't walk with us when you're a pigeon. It won't look right. And the last thing we want to do is draw attention to ourselves. That means you have to travel in the rucksack.'

'SQUAWK!'

'We don't have time for this,' I said impatiently. 'Do you want to get turned back into a human or not?'

'SQUAWK!'

'Unless you've figured out how to fly?'

Monsieur Crépeau's eyes bulged at me with indignation.

With annoying slowness, he waddled into the front pocket of my rucksack and wriggled inside until only his head was visible.

Finally.

I swung the rucksack over my shoulder and leapt downstairs, almost crashing into Dad, who was carrying Albertus.

'Sorry, Dad. I'm going to Broccoli's. See you later,' I said, my hand on the door.

'Wait a minute,' said Dad. 'You have to take Albertus with you.'

I froze, my brain *whirring* with a reasonable excuse. 'But he's not allowed round Broccoli's. Not after he ate their plug socket.'

Albertus burbled and smacked his lips in delight.

'Ask Broccoli to come here, then.'

'But—'

'I've got my Online Sudoku Final this afternoon, remember?' Dad's eyebrows waggled at me sternly over his glasses. 'That means you have to look after Albertus.' Before I could say anything else, he put Albertus in my arms and started upstairs. 'And don't let him near the fridge. Last time he ate **all** the mangoes.'

mangoes

'But –' I looked at Albertus. He blinked back at me with his **enormous** amber eyes and licked my face, leaving a **trail of dinosaur spit** along my cheek. I sighed.

'Let's get your Transporter, Albertus,' I said. 'We're going on a trip.'

Broccoli was already outside, his nose stuck in a book titled *Tortoise Inspections Master Guide*.

TORTOISE
INSPECTIONS

MASTER
GUIDE

Archibald was staring at the pages with a look of ultimate **BOREDOM**.

[A note from Broccoli: Like me, Archibald was, in fact, concentrating. Preparing for tortoise inspections is hard work. It is even harder when you are trying to turn your teacher back into a pigeon at the same time.]

Albertus burbled when he saw them, his arms reaching out towards Broccoli's hair.

'What's *he* doing here?' said Broccoli, gently pushing Berty's claws away. His eyes widened as I slid a large megaphone-shaped device into the Transporter's side pocket. 'Is that his *Pooper Scooper Hoover*?' he said incredulously.

(In case you, the Reader, are wondering, this was

not just a Pooper Scooper Hoover. This was a foldable Ultimate Suction Pooper Scooper Hoover with a water spray and blueberry perfume, **invented** by my **genius** self.)

'A genius inventor must always be prepared, Broccoli,' I said wisely. 'I can't risk any – uh **accidents** interfering with our mission.' I passed him the rucksack. 'You'll have to carry Monsieur Crépeau and the RoarEasy.'

'SQUAWK!' said Monsieur Crépeau, glaring at Broccoli as if to say, 'you'd better be careful, boy'.

Albertus grinned and stuck his tongue up his nose.

Broccoli sighed. 'We can't take Berty with us,' he said. 'He's . . .' Monsieur Crépeau raised an eyebrow and swivelled his head expectantly. 'Well – you know.'

'We don't have a choice,' I said. 'We'll just have to keep an eye on him. Besides, you're bringing Archibald, aren't you?'

'The *Tortoise Inspections Master Guide* says that tortoise owners should spend as much time as possible with their tortoise, especially before an inspection,' retorted

Broccoli. 'I can't leave him behind.' He sniffed. 'Besides, the inspection is tomorrow and I'm already behind with his preparation.' Archibald rolled his eyes and stuck his head inside his shell. 'And you can't just change the plan without telling me.'

'Have you forgotten Chapter 21 of the *Inventor's Handbook*?' I snapped impatiently.

Improvisation is genius in motion.

'Esha, I really don't think this is a good—'

began Broccoli again.

(Honestly, he really is such a (worrier) sometimes.)

Fortunately, I was saved from listening to any more of his yawn-boring-yawn flapping by a loud **DING-A-LING-DING**.

My mouth dropped as an orange limousine with pea-green tyres zoomed to a stop in front of us. On top of it was a spinning globe with the words **CENTRAL RESEARCH LABORATORY**.

'Come on, Broccoli!' I said, my inventor's instincts tingling as I pulled him forward.

'But—'

'There's not a moment to waste. We've got a molecular modulator to find!'

The Central Research Laboratory

I am sure that you, the Reader, are b°uncing with
SPINGLY-TINGLY excitement to know what the Central
Research Laboratory looked like, just like I was.

[A note from Broccoli: I am not sure if excitement is quite what
I was feeling.]

Ernie had told me about it a **GAZILLION** times, but I
hadn't paid him any attention — it is very hard to listen to
an **AIR-BRAIN** when your mind is busy with *real* inventing.

Prepare yourself, Reader.

What you are about to see is a

BRAIN-BOGGLING
MIND-MUDDLING
STOMACH-SINGING

SPECTACLE OF

WONDER...

'Broccoli, look,' I whispered as we drove past the entrance. 'There it is. The Central Research Laboratory.'

My inventor's instincts shivered with delight.

'It's even more magnificent than I imagined.'

'Tortoise claws – check length . . .' murmured Broccoli, his nose stuck inside his master guide. 'Archie, did you hear that? Luckily, I brought your tortoise-care pouch with me. It's got a claw ruler inside.'

Archibald, who was tucked away inside Broccoli's pocket, made a noise that sounded like, 'tortoises do not measure their claws, human. We use them'.

[A note from Broccoli: He did not say that.]

'Broccoli, you need to put that book away,' I said impatiently as the limousine stopped next to the edge of the lawn beside an ENORMOUS red postbox marked TOUR DROP OFF. 'We have a mission, remember? Locate the molecular modulator and figure out a way to get to it without being caught. That means you have to keep your ears and eyes op—'

'Clear the way, please!' A man in an orange spacesuit, **thick** goggles and a purple helmet bounced past me on GIANT springs, nearly knocking me into the postbox. 'Out of the way! Forces unit coming through.'

A moment later, a woman in an orange spacesuit hurried past us, holding a trio of balloons. At least, they looked like balloons. Peering closer, I realized that they were, in fact, *HUGE BUBBLES*. Floating inside each one was a person in an orange spacesuit. One was reading a newspaper, another was knitting, one was even drinking a cup of tea. Stamped across the bubbles were the words **PROPERTY OF THE MATTER UNIT**.

Berty poked his head out of the Transporter. His eyes widened as he spotted the bubbles. With a *frightened shriek*, he dived back inside the Transporter, quivering.

[Make sure your T-rex does NOT eat shampoo. They'll be burping bubbles for days afterwards.]

Suddenly the postbox WHIRR-CLICKED to life.

My mouth **dropped** as the door opened and a woman in an orange spacesuit stepped out in front of us. Her hair was bright purple and her eyes, which were hidden behind a pair of thunderbolt-shaped goggles, were bright and curious, like an owl. A badge with different weather symbols was sewn into her suit. 'Hello, younglings!' she said, beaming. Her gaze fell on Archibald. 'And pet. And a sunny, sunny welcome to you all. I am Meteorologist Brenda and I work with the Weather Unit. You must be one of the special winners of our raffle. Congratulations! May I see your tickets? Ah – yes –' she said, checking them against a cloud-patterned console marked REGISTER. 'Number Twelve and Thirteen. Nishi Verma and guest. This way, please.'

Broccoli sneezed loudly.

(He might as well have been wearing a T-shirt that said $\underline{\text{GUILTY}}$.)

We followed her into the postbox. Hanging from the ceiling were two springy handles labelled: DEPARTURE and ARRIVAL.

cirrus cloud →

'Quite the cirrus today,' said Meteorologist Brenda. She tugged the ARRIVAL handle and beamed at us again. 'My favourite cloud. What's yours?' The postbox door clicked shut.

'Oh – I – uh – cumulo – nimbus,' I said. 'It's very – uh – nimbus-y.' (Fortunately, my DRONG of a sister had given me enough **boring** cloud facts to last me a lifetime.)

VHUMP!

The postbox suddenly PLUNGED downwards, knocking all the air out of me. Broccoli flew sideways with a shriek. A loud RAT-TAT-TATTLING filled my ears. Before I had a chance to catch my breath, it came to a swift stop.

'Here are your maps and tour packs,' said Meteorologist Brenda, handing one to each of us. 'They will be collected from you at the end of the tour so please keep hold of them. You're the last to arrive so we'll start immediately,' she continued, striding out.

'Archie, are you OK?' said Broccoli, holding his ~~evil~~

reptile tortoise level with his face. 'You're not feeling dizzy, are you?'

Archibald snickered as if to say, 'let's do that again'.

'Come *on*, Broccoli,' I said, speeding out after Meteorologist Brenda. We were inside a spaceship. At least, it *looked* like a spaceship. From top to bottom, the walls, the ceiling, even the floor were covered in shiny metal panels. Between the panels were at least twenty different silver lifts. They glowed with a green light, each lift WHOOSHING loudly as it took off or landed.

I whistled. 'Those look fast.'

'Absolutely,' said Meteorologist Brenda as more orange spacesuits hurried past us. 'The laboratory is **enormous** so everyone uses the lifts. They're the quickest way to get around. The stairs are only for emergencies.'

I nudged Broccoli, who still had his nose deep inside his book. 'Did you hear that, Broccoli?' I whispered. 'The stairs are our best chance of sneaking around **without being SEEN.'**

In the centre of the lifts was one that looked **different** from all the rest. It was a brilliant sea-blue colour with silvery-white letters on top.

'**Lift X,**' I murmured, reading aloud. 'What's that?'

'To check your tortoise's shell, you must . . .' murmured Broccoli under his breath.

'Oh, that's for the fifth floor,' said Meteorologist Brenda as we followed her to a group of noisy children.

ancient →

Beside them was a man in a pea-green uniform. He was as old as an ancient walrus and his eyes were almost closed, as if he were asleep.

'We keep our **MOST DANGEROUS** experiments and devices up there. Unlike the other lifts, Lift X has been custom-built to be waterproof, electro-resistant, wind-stabilized, etc. Currently, it's the only one that goes to the fifth floor. As you'll see from the map, there are currently seven experiments up there, including the Weather Simulation Room.'

'But **not** the molecular modulator,' I whispered to Broccoli, peering at the map. 'They must be keeping that on a different floor.'

'Gather round, everyone!' shouted Meteorologist Brenda. The pea-green uniform woke with a start. There were nine other children in total, each with a guest. Some of the children were looking at their maps, others were wearing wellingtons or clutching compasses.

'As **winners** of our special raffle, you've all been given a chance to experience an exclusive weather-themed tour of the Central Research Laboratory. Here, we will show you some of the Weather Unit's **special research**. As you know, our tour will end at two o'clock with the grand opening of the Weather Simulation Room, where each of you will be given the chance to **appear on TV.'**

Broccoli (who had FINALLY stopped reading his book) sniffed. 'What happens if Nishi finds out the truth?' he whispered.

'She'll think it was an unfortunate mix-up, that's all,' I hissed back, moving my finger along the key at the side of the map. 'According to this, the molecular modulator isn't on the fourth floor or the third floor.'

The pea-green uniform yawned.

'Before we begin, I must go over a few rules,' said Meteorologist Brenda.

A pair of orange suits wearing weather badges rushed past us, carrying a stretcher between them. 'Quickly – clear the way, please! We have to **DEFROST HIM** before he stiffens up!' On top of the stretcher, his mouth open in shock, was another pea-green uniform, his entire body frozen in ice. 'And we need another snow cylinder in the Weather Simulation Room—'

'Not again,' said Meteorologist Brenda impatiently. 'That's the sixteenth guard this week. They really must learn to be more *careful*.'

There was a ripple of **frightened** murmurs around us.

'Now, where was I?' continued Meteorologist Brenda. 'Ah – yes. **Rule One**: Don't wander off. As you have just seen, the laboratory can be a dangerous place and we don't want any storm clouds spoiling your day.'

Archibald poked his head out of Broccoli's pocket with interest. 'Don't look so worried, Archie,' whispered Broccoli, glancing down at him. 'I won't let anything happen to you.'

'**Rule Two:** DO

NOT

TOUCH

ANYTHING.

The equipment in these rooms is **extremely expensive.**'

Monsieur Crépeau warbled impatiently.

I frowned. 'I can't see the molecular modulator here AT ALL.'

'So how do we find it?' whispered Broccoli.

'**Rule Three:** Anyone found breaking these rules will be **automatically ejected** from the tour and the laboratory. **Rule Four:** Keep hold of any pets or other important items. **Rule Five:** Photography of any kind is **strictly forbidden.** Now, our first stop on the tour is the Wind Turbine Room,' she continued. 'Any questions before we begin?'

I put up my hand. 'Will we also be seeing the molecular modulator?'

Meteorologist Brenda blinked. 'The molecular modulator?' she said blankly. 'I'm afraid I don't know what you're talking about. We have many different experiments and devices here; only **Professor Rathbone**, the Head of Research, knows about **all** of them.'

'It's on loan to the laboratory from India,' I said. I held the map up. 'I can't see it on here.'

'Loans and borrowings are not included on the map. Information regarding the laboratory's loans and borrowings, including their floor location, is kept in the library. Unfortunately, that will **not** be included in the tour today. Any more questions?' Another child put up their hand. 'Yes?'

'**Now what?**' said Broccoli. 'Finding out where they're keeping the molecular modulator was supposed to be the **easy** part of the plan.'

I glanced at the map again. 'Look, there's the library – on the first floor.' I folded the map and slipped it into my pocket. 'We get away from the tour, head to the library and figure out which floor the molecular modulator is on.

We find it, change Monsieur Crépeau and get back before anyone realizes we're missing. Simple.'

Broccoli sniffed. 'That's what you said about getting Nishi back. And we got swallowed by a Guzzler.'

'We escaped, didn't we?' I reminded him sharply.

'Esha?' called a familiar **weaselly** voice behind me.

My inventor's instincts tingled to **RED ALERT** as I turned round.

My mouth dropped.

It couldn't be.

There, on the other side of the hallway, was the very last person I wanted to see at that moment.

Ernie Rat-Bone.

My ARCH-NEMESIS.

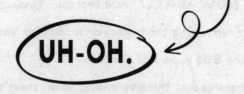

He stared at us in confusion.

'Ernie,' whispered Broccoli. His snot dropped a centimetre.

This was absolutely not good. In fact, on a disaster scale of one to ten, this was **ONE HUNDRED**. After all, I hadn't factored facing down my **ARCH-NEMESIS** into the plan.

Ernie was already heading in our direction, his skateboard puffing green smoke behind him.

Broccoli sneezed. 'What do we do?' he whispered.

Monsieur Crépeau peered up from the rucksack, blinking at us as if to say, 'would someone like to tell me what's going on?'.

'Act normal,' I whispered back. 'We're here for the tour, remember?'

'Hello, **WORMS**,' said Ernie, whizzing to a stop in front of us. 'What are you doing here?'

'None of your business,' I snapped.

He glanced at the ticket in my hand.

'I didn't know **YOU** were a raffle winner,' he said, his eyes NARROWING in suspicion.

'You don't know a lot,' I said.

Broccoli sniffed.

There was a low *chuk-chuk* noise from his pocket, which sounded like Archibald laughing.

Fortunately, at that moment, Meteorologist Brenda reappeared beside us.

'Hello, Ernie. Are you joining the tour?'

'No,' he scoffed. 'I have far more *important* things to do.'

'Not trialling another invention, I hope,' said Meteorologist Brenda, peering down at him over her glasses. 'Your uncle wasn't impressed with your recent gismo *almost* **flooding** the Cheese Room.'

I sniggered.

Ernie flushed a deep beetroot colour. 'That was an accident,' he growled. 'And it wasn't a gism—'

'Well, there can be no accidents today,' interrupted Meteorologist Brenda. 'Professor Rathbone has been very clear. The *SCIENCE TODAY* TV crew are coming to see the Weather Simulation Room and everything must go perfectly. This is going to be the **BIGGEST** scientific breakthrough of the CENTURY.'

She spun on her heel and waved at us to follow. 'Keep up.'

'You heard her, Rat-Bone,' I sneered.

Ernie scowled. 'This is my uncle's laboratory, Verma,' he hissed. 'I've got eyes and ears on every *millimetre* of this place. Just remember that.'

I could still feel him watching me as we followed the tour across the hallway.

'How are we going to get the molecular modulator now?' Broccoli whispered.

'Ernie doesn't know anything,' I scoffed. 'We stick to the plan. And stop looking so worried, Broccoli. It's just a laboratory. What's the worst that could happen?'

[A note from Broccoli: Quite a lot as it turned out.]

Skunkles and
Supreme Sneakiness

'This way, please,' said
Meteorologist Brenda. She
swiped a purple access card on
a door marked RESTRICTED –

AUTHORIZED ENTRY ONLY. 'The doors are controlled by
a special pass,' she continued. 'In fact, the doors
themselves are made from a special combination of . . .'

The pea-green uniform shuffled beside us, yawning. He
looked so tired that I wouldn't have been surprised if
he'd suddenly dropped to the floor and started snoring.

'Did you hear that, Broccoli?' I whispered as we followed
Meteorologist Brenda past more lifts into a long corridor.
On either side were several doors marked with different
symbols: MATTER UNIT, TEMPERATURE UNIT, GEOLOGY
UNIT. Each one had a peculiar name: MILK-SHAKER –
UMBRELLA FLOATER – MOON DUST. A short way ahead of

us was a door marked **STAIRS: EMERGENCY USE ONLY.**

Exit for emergency use only

'We need to get hold of an access card.'

But my snivelly apprentice wasn't listening. Instead, he was squinting into the air.

Archibald looked up and began **HALOOTING** with glee.

The pea-green uniform took his card out of his pocket, used the edge to scratch his nose, then put it back in his pocket again.

> **BINGO.**

'Broccoli—'

'I'm sure I heard something buzzing,' he interrupted, puzzled. 'Didn't you?'

'No,' I said impatiently.

(How is anyone meant to ~~steal~~ borrow anything when their accomplice isn't paying attention?)

'Now listen to me. I think I know how to get hold of an access card.'

Monsieur Crépeau warbled as if to say, 'what's taking so long?'.

The pea-green uniform yawned.

'We're going to take it. From *him*.'

'How?'

'We'll use the distraction we planned to get away from the tour group. You ready?'

Broccoli nodded and pulled a peg out of his pocket. 'Ready.'

'Here.' I stuck my hand into my Inventor's Kit and passed him a bag marked **DANGER: USE WITH CAUTION.** Inside it was another bag, and inside that, carefully stored in a box, were five **Skunkles**.

(The first prototype had **accidentally**

EXPLODED

at Dadaji's birthday party. The less said about *that* the better.)

'The Wind Turbine Room is at the end of this corridor,' continued Meteorologist Brenda.

The Transporter jerked suddenly. 'Stay, Berty,' I whispered fiercely. 'I'll let you out soon, I promise.'

'I told you we shouldn't have brought him,' said Broccoli. He looked up again. 'Are you *sure* you can't hear buzzing?' he said.

'No, Broccoli,' I snapped.

Monsieur Crépeau warbled again. 'Don't sound so worried, Monsieur Crépeau,' I said, pulling out a peg for myself. 'My – *our* – Skunkles are a **perfectly disgusting**, perfectly disarming diversion. Expertly made from a special formula of six-month-old paneer cubes, an old PE sock, T– *ahem* – lizard vomit—'

paneer cheese

'– and Nishi's \wellington whiff,'/ added Broccoli proudly. 'That was my idea.'

Archibald took one look at the Skunkles and shot into his shell.

Monsieur Crépeau grunted with impatience.

'Keep up, please, everyone,' called Brenda from the front.

'Broccoli, wait for my signal,' I said. Holding the peg in my hand, I shuffled through the tour group until I was next to the pea-green uniform.

'Hurricanes are the **most dangerous** weather event,' chirped one boy. 'Everyone knows that.'

'Not more dangerous than a weathernova,' said another girl. 'Says so right here in my *Destructive Weather Encyclopedia*. See?'

If I hadn't been in the middle of an **important MISSION**, I'm sure my brain would have **melted** from on-the-spot boredom.

When we were a few steps from the staircase, I turned

round and nodded at Broccoli. He whipped the peg over his nose, then, one by one, he pulled out the safety strings from the Skunkles and rolled them across the floor.

'What is tha—' began one of the boys in front.

A moment later, there was a loud HISS as the Skunkles ejected a cloud of purple smoke. It rose around us, thick and warm and **entirely FOUL**.

'IT STINKS!' howled a girl.

'WHAT IS IT?'

'I CAN'T SEE ANYTHING!'

'EVERYONE, PLEASE STAY CALM!' shouted Brenda.

Beside me, the pea-green uniform was bent over, coughing loudly. With one **SUPREMELY SNEAKY** manoeuvre, I slipped the card out of his pocket and pushed past the tour towards Broccoli.

'WOULD YOU PLEASE *STAY CALM?*' shouted Brenda behind us. 'I'M SURE THERE IS A PERFECTLY REASONABLE EXPLANATION FOR . . .'

Glancing over my shoulder to check nobody was watching, I swiped the card against the door and slipped out of the corridor, Broccoli close behind me. Brenda's voice faded away as we sprinted up the stairs.

'This place really is **humongous,**' panted Broccoli, unclipping the peg from his nose. More stairs curled above our heads in a *dizzying spiral.*

'Just keep moving,' I huffed, leaping up the steps.

our footsteps echoing around us . . .

up more
AND MORE stairs . . .

Up we ran . . .

until, at last, we reached a door marked **FIRST FLOOR.**

I bent over to catch my breath. 'The library should be further down this corridor,' I said, checking the map. I placed my hand on the door handle and looked at Broccoli.

His face was shiny with sweat. 'Ready?'

He sneezed. 'Ready.'

Taking a deep breath, I slid the door open a crack and peeped into the corridor. It was empty. 'Clear,' I said, hurrying inside. 'Come on, Broccoli.'

'What if we get caught?' he murmured.

On either side of us were more **thrumming** lifts and peculiar doors with **strange** names. In the distance ahead, I could hear the hum of voices from one of the rooms.

'We're not going to get caught, Broccoli,' I whispered impatiently. 'I've read Chapter 50 of the *Inventor's Handbook*, remember? Stealth is *practically* my middle name.'

Archibald yawned at me rudely.

'And I have a certificate in concealment and camouflage.'

Monsieur Crépeau squawked in surprise.

'Oh, that's a must-skill for **genius inventors**, Monsieur Crépeau.'

(He might have been a guest judge for the Young Inventor of the Year contest, but he *clearly* needed someone to teach him about inventing.)

'I can hear that buzzing again,' murmured Broccoli as we sped along the corridor. 'Strange – I couldn't on the stairs.'

'It comes in very handy when inventions don't always work quite to plan,' I continued. 'In fact, the *Inventor's Handbook* lists hiding as one of—'

Berty's head shot out of the Transporter quicker than a rocket. Before I could stop him, he leapt on to the floor, his claws scraping against the tiles as he sprinted away.

'No, Berty,' I whispered, whirling round. 'We're not playing *hide-and-seek*!'

(OK, I am sure that you, the Reader, are probably wondering how a **genius inventor** such as myself could break my own **golden rule** about T-rexes. That is what you call a SLIP OF THE TONGUE. It is a common side-effect when your brain is filled with other important **genius**.)

'I knew this would happen,' squeaked Broccoli, his snot wobbling as he ran after me. 'T-rexes aren't built for top-secret missions!'

Monsieur Crépeau poked his head out of the rucksack.
His eyes **widened** in **horror**. Archibald grinned, his
wrinkly face bouncing up and down in excitement.

'Come back here, Berty!' I panted, sprinting after him.
Unfortunately, that only made him run faster.

He powered across the floor, his tail flicking in delight.

'Berty!'

My inventor's instincts quivered in warning as I ran
after him. If someone caught us, we'd be EJECTED from the
laboratory and we'd have a MINUS ZERO chance of finding
the molecular modulator and de-birding Monsieur Crépeau.
I leapt towards Berty's tail, but he dived out of my reach
and swerved towards Broccoli, who jumped towards him
and . . . missed.

Monsieur Crépeau warbled in irritation.

'There's nowhere left for you to run, Berty,' I puffed
as he hurtled towards a wall at the end of the corridor.
He stopped with a disappointed whine, then turned back
towards me with a guilty expression on his face. A guilty
expression I knew too well.

'No, Berty,' I said, 'not here. **DON'T -'**

With a happy squeal, Berty POOPED  in front of me.

Broccoli drew to a stop behind me. 'Esha, we have to go –

EURGH!' He clapped a hand to his nose. His eyes widened as I pulled the Pooper Scooper out of the Transporter. 'What are you doing?'

'Well, I can't leave it here, can I?' I retorted. 'If someone finds it, they'll start asking questions.'

I switched the scooper to silent mode and aimed it at the poop.

Broccoli glanced around the corridor, his snot trembling. 'Hurry up, Esha.' He wiggled his finger in his ear. 'What is that buzzing?'

'Done!' I said as the last of the poop disappeared into the scooper. 'That ultimate suction is absolute geni—'

Suddenly Monsieur Crépeau warbled. His head bobbed towards a lift. A moment later, it stopped with a

(((LOUD DING.)))

The Composter

'Oh no,' whispered Broccoli.

'There!' I said, pointing to a door marked **COMPOSTER: CLOSED FOR MAINTENANCE.** On the front was a glass window; beyond it the room was in darkness. 'Looks empty.'

We sprinted towards it, diving inside just as the lift doors swished open behind us.

'It's OK, Archie,' whispered Broccoli. He took out a stopwatch.

I stared at him. 'Broccoli, what are you doing?'

'Measuring Archie's breathing,' he said. 'To check for stress.'

'Now?'

Archibald was staring at Broccoli as if he were the most irritating thing he had ever seen.

'Slightly higher than usual,' said Broccoli with a frown. 'Must be the running.'

Footsteps echoed in the corridor.

'I can still hear that buzzing,' said Broccoli, glancing around in puzzlement.

Ignoring my apprentice, who was **RUDELY** ignoring me, I peered through the window. Berty wriggled in my arms, his claws reaching for the access card. 'That's not for you to eat, Berty – look, you can have this.' I pulled out a handful of toffee popcorn from his Transporter. Unfortunately, despite my excellent distraction technique, Berty dived for the access card at that exact moment, sending it whizzing out of my hands.

Monsieur Crépeau warbled in horror.

'Esha,' whispered Broccoli as I bent down to look for the access card.

I absolutely *could not* hear any more about tortoise breathing rates so I pretended not to hear him.

'Esha, they're coming this way.'

'What?'

I shot up and peeked through the window. Sure enough, two spacesuits were heading in our direction. One was dressed in an orange spacesuit with a badge labelled ENVIRONMENTAL UNIT. The other was wearing a purple spacesuit marked –

OH NO.

'She's from Maintenance,' I said.

Archibald's face wrinkled into a delighted grin.

I spun round and squinted in the darkness for another hiding place. (A note on sneaking around a top-secret laboratory: be prepared to hide **AT ALL TIMES.**)

Through the gloom, I could see a peculiar contraption in the middle of the room. It was built like a huge circular conveyor belt and on the ceiling above it hung an enormous whisk. On top of the belt were three **HUGE** metal pans: each one perfectly big enough to hide a **genius inventor** and an apprentice.

THE COMPOSTER

'In here!' I slid Berty into the Transporter and climbed on to the belt.

'Are you sure?' murmured Broccoli. 'It doesn't look very safe.'

The footsteps were getting **louder**.

'Move!' I snapped.

Grabbing hold of the edge of a pan, I pulled myself up, my feet scrabbling against the sides, and heaved myself inside. Broccoli joined me a moment later, sliding inside with an awkward THUNK.

There was a warble from the opposite end of the room.

I looked at Broccoli, my inventor's instincts quivering. 'Where's Monsieur Crépeau?'

'He's –' Broccoli checked the rucksack, his face paling as he saw that it was empty. 'I don't – he must have slipped out.'

I poked my head over the top of the pan. Monsieur Crépeau was waddling towards us, the access card held in his beak.

'What are you doing?' I hissed. 'I would have got that afterwards.'

Monsieur Crépeau glared at me and continued to waddle forward.

 **EURGH.**

'This is why you should *never bring a teacher* on a mission,' I muttered, clambering out of the pan. Suddenly I heard the echo of voices outside. I froze. Monsieur Crépeau looked at me, his feathery moustache twitching.

'Quick!' I said, scrabbling back into the pan. To my **COMPLETE** bewilderment, he opened his wings, flapped helplessly for a second and fell forward. *Honestly!*

The door handle rattled.

Monsieur Crépeau wobbled upwards with a dizzy squawk.

'Get behind the door, Monsieur Crépeau,' I whispered. 'And keep quiet.'

With a rude warble, he did as he was told.

'Are you sure you can't hear that buzzing?' said Broccoli, looking up into the air.

'No. Now be QUIET.'

'. . . the strangest thing.'

My heart **thudded** as the spacesuits stepped inside. There was the click of a switch and light flooded into the room. I swallowed and tried not to think about what would happen if they caught us here. (Clue: **MAJOR DISASTER.**)

Beside me, Broccoli sniffed, clutching tightly on to Archibald. Berty, who was tucked up in the Transporter, was happily chewing popcorn.

'The composter has been designed to recycle

objects. Take a *rusty tin can*, for example. Put it in the composter and – *boop-de-boop* – at the press of a button, you can recycle it into a pair of *magnificent* earrings. A burst football can become whole again. An old glass bottle can become a window.'

My inventor's instincts tingled in awe. If I hadn't been hiding out of sight, I would've absolutely jumped out to congratulate them on the **MAGNIFICENCE** of this idea. I glanced at Broccoli to check he was making notes. He was not. Instead, my apprentice was *measuring Archibald's claws.* I poked him sharply and pointed above my head, then at his notebook.

Broccoli waved his claw ruler at me and pointed at Archibald.

I glared at him. Clearly, my apprentice had **FORGOTTEN** how to do his job.

[A note from Broccoli: I had not.]

'At least, that's the idea. Instead of composting, it's COMPACTING. Here, let me show you. If we put in this tin of shoe polish and initiate—' There was the *beep-ding-beep* of buttons being pressed. A loud **SCRAPING** noise echoed above us as a metal lid slid over the pan, plunging us into

TOTAL, *toe-tingling* DARKNESS.

Berty whined and dived inside the Transporter.

'**COMPOSTING IN PROGRESS**,' said an automated voice.

OH NO.

'Esha,' squeaked Broccoli. I switched on my inventor's torch. In the glow of the light, Broccoli's eyes blinked back at me like a frightened owl.

'I knew th-this w-was a **b-b-a-a-d i-d-d-e-a-a**,' he stammered in fright, his hand still gripping the claw ruler. 'Th-th-e T-T-or-t-toise Wel-f-a-are Socie-t-t-y wo-uld-d-n't b-be h-h-a-pp-y w-wi-th—'

(((**DING-DING-DING.**)))

'**COMPOSTING COMPLETE – CONTAINER ONE**,' said the voice again.

There was the loud scraping of another lid opening. I breathed out in relief.

'You see,' said the voice, sounding muffled through the metal, 'the tin has COMPACTED.'

'Fascinating,' said the other voice. 'It's completely shrunk.'

'I dropped my glasses inside last week. Luckily the Matter Unit used their **Big-o-Meter** to resize them. We've found you can *reverse* the effects within two hours. After that, the object stays shrunk.'

'Have you checked the control panel?'

'Twice. We still can't figure it out. We think the regolotor must be faulty.'

'I'll have to log it. We're still clearing the third floor after that incident with the Geology Unit. I've never seen such a pebble storm. They've even got into some of the vents . . .'

Their voices faded away, followed by the sound of the door closing. I waited until I was sure they were gone, then I stood up.

'That was close,' breathed Broccoli. He stroked the top of Archibald's head. 'None of this is good for his nerves, you know.'

'He looks fine to me.'

'That's because you don't know anything about tortoises,' said Broccoli with a sniff. 'You should read the *Tortoise Inspections Master Guide*. It's a must for expanding your reptilian expertise.'

YAWN-BORING-YAWN. ⟵

Resisting the urge to tell him exactly what he could do with all his tortoise knowledge, I pushed against the lid.

'It's stuck,' I grunted.

'You should try the Pow-Punch,' said Broccoli.

'I *know* that,' I said impatiently. I took out the Pow-Punch and aimed it at the lid. BOING! It clanged against the metal, which stayed firmly in place.

'It's not **strong** enough,' I grunted. I banged against the metal. 'Monsieur Crépeau? The lid is stuck. Can you get us out of here?'

There was a faint warble followed by silence.

'Monsieur Crépeau? Check the control panel. There must be a way to open the lid.'

He warbled again, louder and more crossly, as if to say, 'what do you think I'm doing?'.

'I knew we shouldn't have hidden in here,' said Broccoli.

'We didn't have a choice,' I pointed out.

'That's because Berty ran off. I *told* you it wasn't a good idea to bring him.'

'COMPOSTING IN PROGRESS,' said the automated voice again.

Only this time, the pan began to *move along the belt.*

I whacked the lid. 'I DON'T THINK THAT'S THE RIGHT BUTTON!'

There was a panicked warble from outside.

BEEP-DING-BEEPITY-BEEP-DING-DING

went the buttons.

'SWITCH IT OFF, MONSIEUR CRÉPEAU!' I yelled.

'SWITCH IT OFF RIGHT—'

All of a sudden, *I was struck by the most* PECULIAR *feeling.*

It was the strangest sensation. My body felt hot and cold at the same time. A loud THRUMMING noise echoed through my ears. My stomach flipped UPSIDE-DOWN. Then my skin began tingling.

'What's happening?' squeaked Broccoli.

I opened my mouth to reply, but the tingling feeling was all over me now; my arms, my legs, even my head, felt as if they were being PULLED tightly downwards by invisible strings.

Tighter and tighter until – POP – the feeling stopped as suddenly as it had started.

A bell rang above us.

'COMPOSTING COMPLETE – CONTAINER TWO,' said the automated voice. The lid above us slid open. The container swivelled sideways and dropped us on to the belt. My legs wibble-wobbled as I stood up.

I breathed in sharply as I looked around.

Everything around me had suddenly, strangely, magnified to

ELEPHANT SIZE.

The pan towered over me like a MOUNTAIN OF METAL. The ceiling was miles away. The conveyor belt stretched on for so long that I couldn't even see where it ended.

Berty poked his head out of the Transporter and blinked at me.

'ESHA!' shouted Broccoli.

That's when I spotted a pair of hands clinging to the edge of the belt.

'HELP ME!'

I darted forward and grabbed hold of my apprentice, dragging him on to the conveyor belt. He collapsed into a snotty heap beside me before swaying to his feet. He gasped as he looked around the room.

'Why has everything grown so ginormous?' he squeaked.

 I cleared my throat, wondering how to tell him. (After all, as a **genius inventor**, I'd already figured out what had happened.)

'Well, technically speaking, I don't think everything else has grown,' I said slowly. 'I think it's more that we've—'

'Shrunk!' shrieked Broccoli.

'**oh no, no, no.'**

He stared up at the pan, then back at himself. 'We've been **COMPACTED!**'

'I know!' I clapped my hands in delight and danced on the spot. 'I think we might be the **first** inventor-apprentice team to be shrunk in all of history.'

'Mum and Dad are going to be **furious** when they see me!' Broccoli paused, his snot wobbling. 'In fact, they probably won't even be able to see me. And what will the T.W.S. say?' His voice was now as shrill as an opera-singing mouse.

Archibald made a noise that sounded like, 'this is even better than travelling through time'.

I cartwheeled across the belt, the **ENORMOUS** room

'Isn't it **INCREDIBLE**, Broccoli?'

Berty let out a mini roar of agreement.

Incredible? Have you forgotten that we need to change Monsieur Crépeau back? How are we going to do that now?'

AH.

My excitement p^opped like a balloon.

'SQUAWK!'

I glanced over to the other side of the room. Monsieur Crépeau was perched over the control panel, his bird eyes blinking at us with rocket speed. I had **never seen** such a huge pigeon in my entire life. 'Monsieur Crépeau, you were supposed to GET US OUT,' I shouted, forgetting about him being a teacher, 'not shrink us! We're on a **TIME-CRITICAL** mission, remember?'

Monsieur Crépeau glared at me in **outrage,** then he waggled his left foot at me as if to say, 'Why don't you try using these feet?'

'Archie's breathing rate is even quicker than before!' muttered Broccoli. 'A tortoise isn't supposed to be this size. It must be the shock!' He looked Archibald in the eye. 'I'm going to fix this, Archie. Don't worry—'

'Will you *STOP panicking?*' I snapped. 'If you'd been listening LIKE ME, you would know there's a **Big-o-Meter** here.' I peered at the map. 'Here it is. The Big-o-Meter.' I traced my finger along the key. 'It's on the – **oh.**'

'What?' said Broccoli.

'Well – uh – it's on the fifth floor,' I said. 'Which is only a very slight complication,' I added quickly. 'We jump into Lift X, **big** ourselves and then we'll crack on with the plan.'

'A slight complication?' echoed Broccoli. 'We're tiny!

How are we going to get around like this?' He gasped, his face paling. 'And if we don't big ourselves in two hours we'll stay this size FOREVER.'

I snorted. 'Just because we've shrunk, doesn't mean we can't—'

Before I could finish speaking, the door opened again.

Only this time it wasn't any spacesuits.

It
was
a

ROBOT.

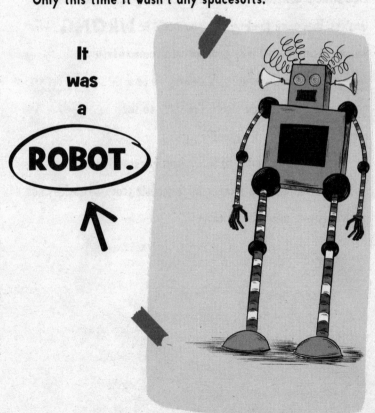

A ~~warning~~ note from Broccoli

Dear Reader, if you have read our first journal you might be thinking that what follows next will be **less terrifying** than dinosaurs and Guzzlers. If you are thinking this, you would be **WRONG.** What you are about to read may send you into uncontrollable sneezes. If, like me, you are still training to be a genius inventor, then you should, I'm sorry to say, continue (with plenty of tissues).

If you are not training to be a genius inventor, you may wish to close this book and read another, more sensible story, which does not involve pigeons, robots or shrinking.

A Complication

I GOGGLED.

Berty took one look at the robot and dived into the Transporter.

'What is that thing?' whispered Broccoli, his eyes **widening**.

The robot marched into the room, its metal legs **CLANKING** loudly. It was about the height of a TALL fridge with glowing green eyes and a wide metal face.

'Searching,' it said. 'Searching –'

Its voice echoed across the room in a mighty metallic rasp. My inventor's instincts tingled in wonder. This metal marvel was a talking robot. Suddenly its eyes fell on the conveyor belt. They flashed twice. 'Targets identified – **targets** –'

Targets?

'Does it mean us?' whispered Broccoli.

Before I could answer, the robot **CLANKED** towards us.

'<u>RUN, BROCCOLI!</u>' I yelled.

We spun round and skittered across the conveyor belt.

'SQUAWK-SQUAWK!' said Monsieur Crépeau, wobbling across the control panel towards us.

BEEP-DING-BEEP.

His feet pushed more buttons. Suddenly the conveyor belt rattled to life again, only this time it was moving backwards.

'What – is – he – doing?' panted Broccoli as we sprinted on the belt.

'MONSIEUR CRÉPEAU, STOP TRYING TO HELP US!' I shouted, glancing back over my shoulder. The robot was only a few steps away from us now.

'SQUAWK!'

Monsieur Crépeau tripped on the control panel, lost his balance and bounced across a few more buttons on to the floor.

BEEP-DING-BEEP.

The conveyor belt spun round at HYPER SPEED.

We flew into the air and bounced along the belt.

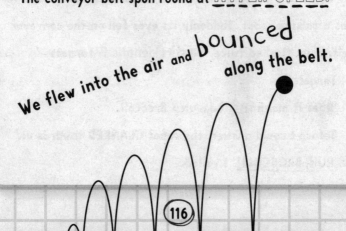

THUD! THUMP! THUNK!

'Ow,' groaned Broccoli, landing beside me.

CLANK CLUNK.

Out of the corner of my eye, I saw a metal hand reach out towards me. Before I could move, I felt myself being lifted into the air.

'Oh no, you don't,' I muttered. Scrabbling in my Inventor's Kit for the Pow-Punch, I aimed it at the robot's metal fingers. KERZING! It shot out and . . . dangled in the air, miles away from his hand.

Oh.

'Leave her— **AAARGGH!**' shouted Broccoli as the robot lifted him into the air alongside me. Archibald's head bobbed in delight. 'The floor!' he shrieked. 'It's miles away!'

'LET GO OF US, TIN-HEAD!' I yelled.

'Correction,' said the robot, holding me level with its face. 'My head is not made of tin. It is made from a special alloy of iron and chromium and—'

'I DON'T CARE!' I shouted. 'BERTY!'

At the sound of his name, Albertus poked his head out of the Transporter.

'Get him, Berty!' I shouted.

Albertus blinked at the robot, then dived back inside, the top of his tail quivering. I sighed. So much for being the **most terrifying** reptile IN ALL OF PREHISTORY.

'SQUAWK! SQUAWK!'

Glancing below, I saw Monsieur Crépeau charge at the robot's foot. Head down, he waddled forward with impressive speed, his beak aimed at the metal.

BOING!

He hit the robot so hard that he bounced right back again. (Ow.)

I looked up at the robot with my most FEARSOME face (specifically designed for DRONGS and AIR-BRAINS).

'My name is Esha Verma and I order you to put me down **IMMEDIATELY!**'

The robot blinked, its enormous metal eyes creaking with the movement. A flap on its chest opened with a low hiss. In one quick movement, the robot d
r
o
p
p
e
d me inside.

Monsieur Crépeau squawked dizzily.

'OI!' I shouted, springing to my feet. 'ARE YOU LISTENING? PUT ME—'

'ESHAAAAA!'

I dived out of the way as Broccoli landed with a **THUMP** beside me.

'Targets acquired,' said the robot. 'Proceed.'

The flap hissed shut. With a loud **CLUNK**, the robot turned on the spot and began walking, carrying us away with it.

'This is bad,' whimpered Broccoli through the gloom. The only light came from a thin slit in the centre of the flap above us. 'This is **very bad.**'

I suppose he was sort-of-maybe right. After all, being **ROBO-NAPPED** had not been part of my plan to turn Monsieur Crépeau back into a human.

(Broccoli has pointed out that being COMPACTED was also not part of the plan. I have reminded him that this was an unfortunate incident that nobody could have predicted.)

Broccoli squinted at his watch. 'We've got less than two hours to big ourselves.

Where do you think it's taking us?' he whispered, his snot dangling to **PANIC MODE** as we **CLANKED** and **CLUNKED** forward. With each robotic step, we bounced and jolted sideways, Archibald's wrinkly grin growing wider and **wider**.

[A note from Broccoli: It was not. Like me, Archibald was still recovering from being shrunk to the size of a sunflower seed.]

Berty whimpered, his tail quivering with fright.

I leapt up towards the slit but it was too far away.

'Here,' said Broccoli. He cupped his hands, grunting as I stepped on to them to peer out through the opening.

'What can you see?' he whispered.

'We're inside a lift,' I said. **CLANK CLUNK.** I swayed sideways as the robot swivelled round towards a panel of shiny green buttons with different labels: **BASEMENT TEN – GROUND FLOOR – FLOOR 1,** all the way to **FLOOR 4.** At the top of the panel, in silvery blue letters, gleamed a note that read:

FOR FLOOR 5
PLEASE USE
LIFT X

The robot's metal hand reached out and jabbed **FLOOR 2.**

'The second floor. That means there are only
THREE floors between us and the Big-o-Meter.'
(A **genius inventor** must always focus on the BRIGHT
side.)

'Have you forgotten that we're stuck inside a robot?'
retorted Broccoli unhelpfully.

He really could be very miserable sometimes.

[A note from Broccoli: I didn't have much to be happy about.]

There was a **WHOOSH** as the lift soared upwards. A few
seconds later, it stopped with a loud **DING**.

'We're here,' I said. Only I had no idea where 'here' was.
All I could see through the slit was a long corridor. Men and
women in orange spacesuits darted around us, every single
one of them ignoring the enormous **ROBOT**.

'What do you think it's going to do to us?' whimpered
Broccoli.

'I can't tell exactly where,' I said, pretending not to
hear him. The last thing I needed was for my apprentice to
enter **PANIC MODE**. Not when we still had to:

① Escape a mysterious robot.
② Big ourselves.

(121)

③ Find the molecular modulator and **change** Monsieur
   Crépeau.

④ Get back to the tour group and pretend we'd been
   there the **entire time**.

'Maybe it thinks we're food,' whispered
Broccoli. He sniffed. 'Or maybe it's going
to turn us into tiny robot people— **AAA–**'

I wavered as he wobbled beneath me, both of us
swaying back and forth and up and down.

'–A**A**–'

'Broccoli, keep—'

'–**CH**ooo!'

'– still!'

I tumbled down, groaning as I landed on top of him.

Suddenly, the flap hissed open. A robotic hand lifted us
into the air and dropped us on to a table.

'Ow. Do you mi—'

Before I could finish speaking, a glass jar
was suddenly put over us. I scowled at the
face on the other side.

'Ernie?' squeaked Broccoli.

'Well, **well, well,**' he smirked. 'Who do we have here?'

I glared at Ernie through the glass, my whole body FIZZING with annoyance.

'Let us go, Rat-Bone,' I hissed.

'I can't hear – hang on.' He stuck a pink mushroom-shaped device on to the jar. 'That should do the trick. What did you say?'

'I said, LET US GO!' I shouted furiously, my voice booming through the device.

'Hm – let me think about that. NO.' His smirk widened as he looked me up and down. 'I can't believe you got yourself COMPACTED. Now you really are a couple of worms, aren't you?'

'We didn't do it on purpose,' I snarled.

'Where are we?' sniffed Broccoli, looking around.

'Oh, this.' Ernie stepped back and swept his arms out either side of him. 'This is my Inventor's Workshop. Where I do all my genius thinking, trialling and inventing. My uncle gave it to me.'

I glanced around in puzzlement. I had expected Ernie's workshop to be something spectacular. Instead, it looked a lot like my Inventor's HQ – aka my bedroom (minus the sock mountains).

Opposite us was a desk covered with neat piles of inventing equipment: pipes, nuts, bolts, test tubes, coils, **GENIE** safety goggles and the **GENIE** toolbox, exactly like I had at home (except a little tidier). To our left were three boxes marked: 2.0: Spare Parts, Pincer Pinch — Hooks and Floating Lanterns. To our right was an old computer. Behind Ernie were shelves stacked with trophies marked ERNIE RATHBONE. I blinked in surprise. Ernie had boasted about them a **GAZILLION** times, but I'd never actually believed him.

Underneath the table were **FOUR enormous boxes,** each one labelled with the same note: Inventions to show Uncle Rathbone.

'When I start working with my uncle, I'll share his workshop,' continued Ernie. 'As soon as I win the Young Inventor of the Year contest. You've already met *my* entry.' He waved at the robot. '2.0. A **walking, talking robot** with built-in AI and detachable parts. He's fitted with sensors, cameras and multiple connection ports. Guaranteed to WIN the Brain Trophy.' GUARANTEE

2.0 nodded, his metallic head creaking, his green eyes flashing. 'Pleased to meet you,' he rasped in that same peculiar tinny voice.

Broccoli sneezed again.

My heart dropped to the ends of my toes.

2.0 was Ernie's entry to the contest?

'I sent him down to get you,' continued Ernie. He paused and gave me a **venomous glare**. 'I would have come myself, but that would have been **far** less fun.' His smirk widened. 'Do you want to know how I found you?'

'Don't care,' I said, yawning loudly.

'Buzz-bot,' said Ernie. He dropped a tiny robotic device in front of the jar. It had thin, wiry wings and looked exactly like a wasp. 'Equipped with a

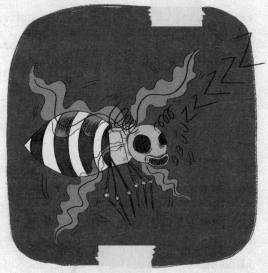

camera and microphone. Suitable for all forms of spying.'

'I was right!' said Broccoli. 'I knew I could hear buzzing.'

'You moved too quickly for me to follow you on the stairs,' said Ernie, 'but I activated another buzz-bot as soon as I realized you were on the first floor. I told you that I've got eyes and ears everywhere. That's how I know you've turned Monsieur Crépeau into a pigeon.' He grinned. 'I knew you were up to something when I saw you downstairs. You're trying to change him back.'

 I glared at him in silence, my brain *whirring* as I tried to remember exactly what I'd said since we'd encountered Ernie in the hall. Did he know about the molecular modulator already?

'Do you have the pigeon, 2.0?' said Ernie.

'Affirmative,' said 2.0.

There was a loud hiss as a second, larger flap on his chest opened.

Monsieur Crépeau blinked at us as 2.0 brought him out and placed him inside a cage. A large bump was starting to form on his head.

Ernie stared at him in fascination. 'He really is a pigeon,' he said. 'How did you do it?' he asked, looking down at me. For one peculiar moment, I was almost sure that he looked impressed. Then I remembered that I was talking to my **AIR-BRAINED ARCH-NEMESIS**.

I folded my arms across my chest and shrugged. No way was I going to tell Rat-Bone anything.

Ernie's eyes narrowed. 'It doesn't matter,' he said haughtily. 'The more important question is how to turn him back. Why did you bring him to the laboratory?'

So he didn't know about the molecular modulator.

'You're a **genius inventor**, aren't you?' I snapped, giving him my best **ESHA LASER GLARE**. 'Why don't you figure it out?' I paused and looked up at him sweetly. 'Unless that's too difficult for you?'

Ernie's eyes narrowed again. 'Oh, I'll figure it out,' he said. 'I don't need you to tell me anything, Verma. See this?' He waved an orange USB device at us and stuck it into a slot on the keyboard. 'This lets me search the laboratory's database. I can read up about experiments and devices, see which floor they're on if I want to have a look at them; when I work with my uncle, my inventions will be recorded on here too.'

The computer hummed.

'ERNIE RATHBONE – ACCESS GRANTED.'

'I can find out how to turn Monsieur Crépeau back into human form quicker than you can say pigeon.' He tapped the keyboard. 'Then I'll change him back in front of the TV crew.'

'TV crew?' Sniffed Broccoli.

Monsieur Crépeau's head shot up.

'Oh, yes,' said Ernie with an EVIL grin. 'I'm going to tell **everyone** that you turned Monsieur Crépeau into a pigeon. Then I, Ernie Rathbone, will turn him back into a human on ☆ ★ LIVE TV.'

The computer *whirred*. 'Everyone will see what a genius I am. Including my uncle. And that's before **I win the contest.**'

Monsieur Crépeau's feathery moustache twitched. Somehow, I don't think the idea of being turned back into a human on live TV was exactly what he'd had in mind for his (STAR) role.

'Imagine it!' Ernie held his fist to his mouth as if it were a microphone and dropped into a TERRIBLE reporter voice. 'Ernie

Rathbone, **genius inventor**, became a _HERO_ when he rescued his teacher and **GENIE** guest judge from another contestant—'

I snorted. 'It was an accident!'

'Doesn't matter. You'll still be disqualified,' he said, his eyes gleaming with menace. 'And everyone will find out why silly girls shouldn't be **inventors**.'

'SQUAWK!' said Monsieur Crépeau, his bird eyes bulging at Ernie in disbelief.

'But – but –' stuttered Broccoli beside me as he peered up at Ernie. 'You can't . . .'

An ice-cold shiver ran over me. He was right – if he revealed that I'd turned Monsieur Crépeau into a pigeon on live **TV**, that would be it. GENIE would know. Mum and Dad would know. I'd **never** be able to invent again.

TAppITY TAP.

'NO INFORMATION FOUND,' said the computer.

Ernie frowned.

TAppITY TAP.

'NO INFORMATION FOUND,'

said the computer again.

TAppITY TAppITY TAP.

'NO INFORMATION FOUND.
NO INFORMATION FOUND. NO INFO—'

'OK!' shouted Ernie. He thought for a moment, **drumming** his fingers impatiently on the keyboard.

I grinned, the DOOMING feeling lifting a little off my shoulders.

'What's the matter, Ernie?' I said slyly. 'Can't you work it out?' I gave him my best SMUG smile. 'Or do you need my help?'

Ernie snorted. 'I'd rather eat a bowl of belly-button fluff.' He checked his watch. 'Less than two hours until the TV crew get here.' Placing a book on top of the glass jar, he whipped off the mushroom-shaped device and leapt to his feet. 'Guard the door, 2.0,' he said as he darted past the robot. 'I'm going to see my uncle. I'll be back soon.'

'Affirmative, Master Rathbone,' said 2.0. His green eyes flashed at us, then he turned on the spot and marched out of the door – **CLANK CLUNK** – shutting it behind him with a **loud**

BANG.

The Great Gumdrop Escape

'I told you he was trouble,' declared Broccoli. He sniffed, and glanced at the walls of the jar around us. 'This is even worse than the Guzzler.'

'Oh, I wouldn't say that,' I said, my inventor's instincts tingling in delight as I looked at the computer. Ernie had left so quickly that he'd forgotten his orange USB device inside it.

'In case you need reminding, we're the size of ants, we can't tickle our way out of this jar and now we have to deal with Ernie too,' huffed Broccoli. He checked his watch. 'And if we don't resize ourselves soon we'll stay this way **FOREVER!**'

I snorted. 'Don't be ridiculous, Broccoli. We might be tiny, but that doesn't mean we can't have **BIG** ideas.'

'SQUAWK!' said Monsieur Crépeau, blinking at us from the cage. The bump on his head had started to turn a nasty shade of green. For a moment, I almost felt sorry for him.

'Don't worry, Monsieur Crépeau,' I said brightly. 'Ernie might think he's a **genius**, but he is, in fact, an AIR-BRAIN. We won't let him turn you back on live TV. That would be a *disaster* for us *all*.'

'SQUAWK!' said Monsieur Crépeau, nodding furiously. 'In fact, you'll be pleased to know that

I have a

GENIUS idea.'

'Like your idea of hiding inside the composter?' said Broccoli sourly.

I ignored him and pointed to Ernie's computer. 'Rat-Bone left his **USB** device behind. That means *we can check the database for the floor location of the molecular modulator*.'

'We can't do **anything** until we're out of this jar,' said Broccoli.

'I know that,' I said impatiently. Trust my apprentice to focus on the part of my idea that was still IN PROGRESS. 'I'm working on it.'

I turned my attention to the book balanced on top of the jar. It really did look very heavy. Placing my hands against the glass, I pushed with all my might. **Nothing**.

'Broccoli, help me move this thing,' I said. 'Even if we can't topple it, we might be able to **push** the jar to the edge of the table. Then we can slip out the bottom.'

He sniffed loudly. 'Do you really think that will work?'

'We won't know if we don't try,' I said. 'Come on.'

We pushed against the jar, but it would **NOT budge.**

'This isn't working,' declared Broccoli with a sniff.

'No,' I snapped. I pulled the Pow-Punch out of my Inventor's Kit and aimed it at the top of the jar. Maybe I could **BOP** the book off the top.

It zoomed upwards and punched the jar.

Not a single shake. Not one wobble.

I scowled. The Pow-Punch wasn't as effective as I'd thought it would be. The **Extend-a-Hand** had been MILES better. (Unfortunately, Berty had eaten the last one.) Monsieur Crépeau warbled in dismay. Waddling forward, he stuck his beak through the cage, trying to unhook the latch.

I peered inside my Inventor's Kit. 'There has to be something else we can use in here. We can't let Rat-Bone get the better of—'

'Floating lanterns,' murmured Broccoli, peering at the box on the other side of the jar. He scratched his head thoughtfully. 'If we can't move the jar sideways, maybe we can move it upways instead.'

I snorted. 'What are you talking about? We don't have a lantern.'

'What about the **Expanding Gumdrops?**' he said, his snot quivering. 'Don't you remember when we trialled them? I accidentally floated on to the shed roof!'

Archibald snickered as if to say, 'what a wonderful day that was'.

'If we stick them to the top of the jar, we might be able to lift it off us. We can create a floating lantern of our own!'

I blinked, my **inventor's instincts** trembling in excitement. Of course.

~~Why hadn't I thought of that?~~

'That's exactly what I was going to say!' I said. I stuck my hand into the bottom of my Inventor's Kit and pulled out a paper bag. Wrapped inside it were five perfectly round, perfectly squidgy gumdrops. 'In fact, I was just about to suggest it.'

'SQUAWK!' said Monsieur Crépeau,

his face fierce with concentration as he jabbed the latch.

I pulled out the safety tag from the first gumdrop, stuck it on top of the Pow-Punch and aimed it at the top of the jar. Before I could hit the release button, Berty stuck his head out of the Transporter and dived towards my hand.

'No, Berty!' I shouted. 'Those aren't for you to eat!' With **genius** quick-thinking, I threw the Pow-Punch and bag of gumdrops towards Broccoli. Berty lunged forward.

'Oh no you don't,' I said, grabbing hold of him.

Broccoli aimed the Pow-Punch upwards.

SPLAT! The first gumdrop stuck to the glass ceiling. Berty bounced in my arms, his body weight pulling against me.

'Hurry up, Broccoli,' I panted, my arms burning. 'Berty's . . . heavy.'

'I'm *trying*,' said Broccoli as the Pow-Punch zipped back down towards him.

SPLAT! went the second gumdrop.

SPLAT! SPLAT! went the third and fourth.

With a loud roar, Berty suddenly lurched out of my hands and shot towards Broccoli.

'Stop it, Berty!' he squealed, jumping out of his path. 'That's not for you!'

The Pow-Punch slipped in Broccoli's fingers, sending the fifth gumdrop sailing through the air. With EYE-POPPING acrobatics, Berty leapt towards it and – BOING – using the Pow-Punch, Broccoli knocked it upwards, out of reach of Berty's jaws.

SPLAT!

'We really shouldn't have brought him,' huffed Broccoli as the fifth gumdrop hit the glass ceiling. Berty looked up at the gumdrop and licked his lips sadly. 'T-rexes aren't designed for—'

There was a loud whooshing noise above us.

'Broccoli, look,' I whispered, pointing upwards.

The first gumdrop was bulging outwards with a loud HISS. The others did the same, each one ballooning out and up with a great rush of air. The book rattled as the gumdrops pushed against the top of the jar, slowly at first, then faster, until the book fell off with a bone-bouncing THUMP.

'Get down!' I said as the gumdrops continued to expand, 'or we'll get stuck!'

We dropped flat on the table, the gumdrops hissing as they puffed out. The jar shook as it rose into the air, lifting UP AND AWAY.

'Ha!' I leapt up and punched the air in delight. We were free. 'Take that, Rat-Bone!'

'I knew it!' exclaimed Broccoli. 'I knew it would work.'

Archibald grunted in annoyance.

'SQUAWK!' said Monsieur Crépeau as if to say, 'is anyone going to help me?'.

'Esha, give me the Pow-Punch,' said Broccoli. He darted towards the cage, the teensy-tiny contraption bouncing under his arm. 'I'm coming, Monsieur Crépeau!'

I sprinted towards Ernie's computer. Standing on my tippy-toes, I pulled myself on to the **GINORMOUS** keyboard. Luckily Ernie was such an **AIR-BRAIN** that he hadn't known what he was searching for. 'M,' I muttered, jumping on to the first square. 'O –' I darted between the letters, the keys clacking under my shoe– 'L – E – C – U – L – A – R – M – O – D – U – L – A – T – O – R.'

The computer **beeped** and *whirred*.

'INFORMATION FOUND,' it said.

'MOLECULAR MODULATOR. ON LOAN.

FLOOR LOCATION: BASEMENT THREE. THE POSTAL ROOM.'

(BINGO.)

I deleted the search and leapt off the keyboard, landing with a thump on the table.

BANG!

The jar suddenly **EXPLODED**, gummy scraps splattering through the air in a **sticky fountain of colour**. There was a *whirr* and a **CLUNK** from the other side of the door.

CLANK. CLUNK.

'SQUAWK!' warbled Monsieur Crépeau, glancing at me expectantly as he waddled out of the cage.

Broccoli peered over the edge of the table with a frown. 'How do we get down? It's too high.'

'We're going to fly,' I said, pulling out the latest prototype of our ultra-awesome getaway invention, **THE GO-GLIDER**.

Archibald's eyes lit up in delight, his wrinkly face creasing into a gleeful grin.

'We get into the corridor, find Lift X and ride it all the way to the fifth floor. Once we've bigged ourselves, we can find the molecular modulator. **Simple.**'

Broccoli moved back, shaking his head as he eyed the Go-Glider. 'No – we can't use that. Last time, we landed in that pond—'

'Do you have a better idea?' I hissed.

CLANK. CLUNK.

The door handle twisted.

'Broccoli!' I hissed. 'Do you want to pass the tortoise inspection or not?'

'What about Monsieur Crépeau? He's **too big** to fly on that!'

Monsieur Crépeau warbled in agreement.

'He's a *pigeon*, remember!' I hissed. 'He'll have to use his wings!'

Monsieur Crépeau's moustache twitched in alarm.

The door handle clicked open.

'Time's up!' I shouted, unfolding the Go-Glider.

The wings fluttered open, the fabric, ~~stolen~~

borrowed from one of Mum's saris

shimmering

a brilliant sky blue.

Mum's sari

2.0 blinked, his metal eyes creaking as he saw two tiny humans sprint into action, a pair of wings held between them.

'SQUAWK-SQUAWK!' said Monsieur Crépeau, waddling behind us.

'Steady!' I shouted to Broccoli as we charged towards the edge of the desk, the Go-Glider flapping above us.

'Are you sure about—' he began.

Too late.

As we neared the end of the table, I pushed the **POWER** button. With a loud spurt of the motor, the propellers *whirred,* lifting us into the air.

The Go-Glider Flight

'SQUAWK!' said Monsieur Crépeau, as if to say, 'don't leave me behind!'.

2.0's eyes *whirred* upwards as we rose away from the table. I looked down, my whole body buzzing with SPINGLY-TINGLY delight.

'IT'S WORKING!' I shouted as we whizzed over 2.0's head towards the open door. 'Look, Broccoli! Flying is EVEN better when you're TINY.'

'THGHEHBEHBEUBEBHBE YEWBNBDY,' came the reply.

I glanced sideways to find Broccoli's eyes TIGHTLY SHUT. Archibald poked his head out of his pocket, his face shining with glee.

'SQUAWK!'

Below us, Monsieur Crépeau was peering worriedly over the edge of the table.

'**YOU CAN DO IT**, MONSIEUR CRÉPEAU!' I yelled.
'YOU'RE A BIRD, REMEMBER!'

He shut his eyes, then, with one brilliant bird-sized
leap, he unfolded his wings, threw himself off the table
and . . .
F
E
L
L on to the chair, before **bouncing**
on to Ernie's skateboard.

The turbines roared to life.

I GOGGLED as Monsieur Crépeau KERZOOMED out
of the room, somehow clinging to the skateboard.

2.0's head spun a full 360 degrees as we zipped into the
empty corridor.

'Targets escaping,' he said. 'Acquire targets.' With
surprising speed, his body swivelled round to match the
direction of his head.

'SQUAWK!' shrieked Monsieur Crépeau as the
skateboard whizzed towards the wall, a cloud of green
smoke puffing behind it. 'SQUAWK! SQUAWK!'

I braced myself, absolutely certain that Monsieur Crépeau was
about to become a pigeon PANCAKE, when, with jaw-dropping

quickness, he threw himself off the skateboard, bouncing across the floor until he landed in a feathery heap.

(Ouch.)

The skateboard slammed against the wall with a loud BANG.

CLANK CLUNK.

I glanced over my shoulder. 2.0 powered after us, his whole body clank-clunking as he marched forward.

'W-w-h-a-t's h-a-p-p-e-n-i-n-g?' squealed Broccoli.

'OPEN YOUR EYES!' I bellowed. '2.0 is chasing us! We have to go faster!'

'Is that really necessary?' he howled.

'There's Lift X!' I shouted, squinting through the smoke at a shiny blue door ahead. 'We have to get close enough to the call button for me to punch it!'

'Tortoises aren't meant to fly!' chattered Broccoli.

CLUNK CLUNK.

'I'll have to time it!'

CLUNK CLUNK.

'This isn't good for Archibald's stress levels!'

CLUNK CLUNK.

'The JET JUMP only lasts a few seconds.'

CLUNK CLUNK.

2.0 was only a few steps away from us now. His green eyes blinked at us with double-speed. 'Target locked,' he said. 'Speed mode engaged.' He spurted forward, his metallic arms clanking as he reached out towards us.

'**NOW!**' I shouted, pressing the JET JUMP button. With a loud POP of the motor, the propellers KERZOOMED us forward, past 2.0's metallic fingers – along the corridor – towards the lift. The Transporter trembled against my back as Berty poked his head out, squealing.

'SQUAWK!' said Monsieur Crépeau, his pigeon eyes following us as we zipped over him. With an exasperated warble, he rolled on to his feet and waddled after us, 2.0 close behind him.

'We're almost there!' I shouted, my cheeks flapping against the whoosh of air. 'Hold on, Brocc—'

Suddenly a door to the left of us opened.

'And that, children, is the Cloud Chamber,' said Meteorologist Brenda, her face looming in front of us. 'The first fully automated cloud-creation chamber in the world.'

'**HRUHJSHJHJHEU!**' mumbled Broccoli as we flew towards her GINORMOUS mouth. We were so close that I could see the gleaming whites of her teeth, the spit pooling on her enormous tongue . . .

'Not this time!' I exclaimed, swerving past her. 'I've been guzzled once alread—'

'That was incredible!' exclaimed a girl, appearing in front of me. 'The cirrus was my favourite! Especially when it floated into the extractor—' She waved a book in the air, knocking the Go-Glider so hard that we spun sideways.

'ESHAAAAA!' shrieked Broccoli. Something zinged out of his pocket. 'NO!' he shouted, nearly letting go of the Go-Glider to jump after it. 'NOT MY TORTOISE-CARE POUCH!'

'STOP IT, BROCCOLI!' I yelled. 'YOU'RE GOING TO MAKE US CRA—'

Too late.

We **smashed** against a boy's cap, the Glider's left wing snapping with a stomach-curling CRACK. My teeth rattled as the cap swivelled sideways, *flinging* us back into the air.

'WE'VE LOST **CONTROL!**' I yelled. '**HOLD ON!**'

'WHAT DO YOU THINK I'M DOING?' yelled Broccoli.

We dipped and swerved, the glider twisting across the corridor like a Catherine wheel. The Pow-Punch flew out of my pocket and tumbled to the ground. The ceiling and corridor flipped before my eyes –

UP,

DOWN,

SIDE

to

SIDE.

I spotted Monsieur Crépeau waddling around the tour group, who were all staring, open-mouthed, at 2.0.

CLUNK CLUNK!

'Oh – 2.0,' said Meteorologist Brenda, her voice echoing haughtily around us. 'You're awfully squeaky today.' She turned towards a lift, still muttering to herself. 'I don't know why Professor Rathbone gave permission for such a sloppy gismo to stomp around the laboratory. This way, please, everyone.'

'THIS WAS A BAD IDEA!' screamed Broccoli.

Archibald chuk-chukked with excitement as we *whizzed*

through the air,

ROUND

and

ᗡᑎՈОᴚ over the tour group

and the pea-green uniform (still yawning),

through the open door,

→ until we landed

with an

ENORMOUS SHLOP

inside an

EVEN

MORE

ENORMOUS

FISHBOWL.

The Cloud Chamber

The door slammed shut behind us.

'What *is* this stuff?' squealed Broccoli. 'It's cold!'

Inside the bowl was a purple liquid. It was gooey like treacle, strangely springy, and we had landed UP TO OUR KNEES IN IT. Outside the bowl was an enormous circular room with a giant black device on the wall. Next to it were three lights, marked INITIATE – READY – GO. The other walls were made from a green foamy material, and hanging down from the ceiling was a huge metal device marked CLOUD EXTRACTOR.

Suspended in the air, several metres above the ground, was a complex network of fishbowls held in the air by thick ropes. Each bowl contained a different amount of purple liquid – the same liquid that we were floating in. On the wall above the black device was a sign that read:

'I can't believe I lost my tortoise-care pouch,' murmured Broccoli. He sniffed. 'You should have flown the Go-Glider more carefully!'

'It's not my fault I had to take **evasive** action,' I retorted. 'And I wasn't the one who made us crash!'

Broccoli ignored me and peered worriedly at the liquid, Archibald held high above his head. 'Do you think this is dangerous to tortoises?'

'How would I—'

'SQUAWK!' interrupted Monsieur Crépeau sternly, as if to say, 'will you two focus?'.

A loud **DING-A-LING-DING** echoed across the room.

'CLOUD INITIATION IN FOUR MINUTES,' said an automated voice.

'Quick, Broccoli!' I said, wriggling out of the broken Go-Glider. I had no idea what cloud initiation involved, but I wasn't going to stick around to find out. We wiggled sideways towards the edge of the bowl and reached up. Just as our fingers met the top, the liquid pulled us back down again with a loud **SHLURP**.

'It's too sticky!' squealed Broccoli.

CLUNK CLUNK.

2.0's face appeared at a round window in the middle of the door. His green eyes flashed as they peered inside. The door rattled.

'ACCESS DENIED. ACCESS CARD REQUIRED.'

'SQUAWK!' said Monsieur Crépeau, flapping his wings at us in impatience.

'Give us a second,' I snapped, shoving my hand into my Inventor's Kit. 'I know I have them here some— *aha!*'

'CLOUD INITIATION IN THREE MINUTES.'

I pulled out the fourth prototype of our jaw-droppingly **BRILLIANT** Gecko Gloves and slapped one against the wall.

SQUELCH.

It stuck on immediately.

Gripping on to the wall, I reached above my head with the other glove. **SQUEL**— With a loud **SCHOOP**, the liquid pulled me back down again, dragging the glove across the glass.

CLANK CLUNK.

'You need to increase the **STICK** setting,' said Broccoli, glancing at the door.

'I know,' I snapped. I slipped off a glove and nudged the STICK setting to SUPREME STICK, using my free hand.

There was a slow *whirr* as the gloves began readjusting.

'SQUAWK!' said Monsieur Crépeau, staring worriedly at the door. A peculiar scraping noise seemed to be coming from the other side. A moment later, A ROBOTIC HAND crawled beneath it and entered the room.

'What – is – that?' gasped Broccoli.

Archibald made a noise that sounded like, 'this just keeps getting better'.

'Detachable parts,' I murmured. Rat-Bone might have been my ARCH-NEMESIS, but I couldn't help feeling a teensy-tiny bit impressed at his invention. 'I think that's 2.0's hand.'

'HIS HAND?' echoed Broccoli in horror.

[A note from Broccoli: I am still not quite sure how I didn't faint at that particular moment.]

The robotic hand flipped itself upright and scuttled towards a control panel on the side of the room.

'Stop it, Monsieur Crépeau!' I shouted. 'It's going to open the door!'

With an alarmed SQUAWK, Monsieur Crépeau shot after it, his feet slapping clumsily across the floor. The hand hopped on to a pile of books – then a chair – before landing on the control panel, clumsily followed by a worried-looking Monsieur Crépeau.

'CLOUD INITIATION IN ONE MINUTE.'

'MOVE, ESHA!' yelled Broccoli.

'I can't,' I snapped. 'The gloves are still readjusting!'

The hand turned round towards Monsieur Crépeau. With the speed of a cannonball, he charged towards it, knocking it sideways. Almost at once, the hand flipped back into an upright position, the fingers tap-tapping on the ground like an animal about to charge. Suddenly it came towards Monsieur Crépeau, who leapt out of the way. Spinning on the spot, he flapped his wings and let out a shrill BATTLE CRY.

The gloves whirred and clicked loudly.

'DONE!' I said, slapping the right one against the bowl.

Another DING-A-LING-DING echoed across the room.

'CLOUD MACHINE INITIATED,' said an automated voice. 'PULSE ONE OF TWO.'

There was a loud *whirr*.

I pressed my face to the glass, eyes **widening** as the lights at the far end of the room changed from INITIATE to READY.

OH NO.

The light changed from READY to GO.

BOOM!

An enormous **wave of energy** suddenly pulsed through the air.

It was so powerful that it made my eyelids flicker at triple speed, jiggled my jawbone and shook my entire body from head to toe. Out of the corner of my eye, I saw Broccoli quaking, his snot swaying like a pendulum. Suddenly the fishbowls around us erupted with a low hissing noise. The liquid at the centre shivered for a moment, then it began to TWIST.

'SQUAWK!' said Monsieur Crépeau, jabbing the robotic hand with his beak.

I grabbed Broccoli's arm.

'HOLD ON, BROCCOLI!' I shouted.

The liquid at the centre was spinning even faster now, round and round, as if someone were sucking it up through an *invisible straw*. The Gecko Glove continued to hold. Around us, the hissing noise was growing louder and **louder** –

'WE'RE GOING TO BE SUCKED IN!' shrieked Broccoli, Archibald grinning over his head.

'IT'S GOING **TOO FAST** –'

Berty poked his head out of the Transporter and squealed.

Just as suddenly as it had started, the hissing stopped. **Then . . .**

With a soft **belching** noise, an ENORMOUS cloud rose out of the centre of the liquid and floated upwards. All around us, the other fishbowls were also burping clouds until there were hundreds of them filling the air. They were all different shapes, some angular and pointed, others domed like jellyfish heads. Their surfaces gleamed a shiny purple colour as they rose up to the ceiling.

A moment later, the device marked **CLOUD EXTRACTOR** turned on with a loud whooshing noise. Broccoli's cheeks flapped. Cool air rushed against my skin as, one by one, the clouds floated towards its enormous mouth and disappeared until there were none left. The cloud extractor continued to make a whooshing noise for a few more minutes before falling silent.

Monsieur Crépeau was now involved in a **BEWILDERING boxing match** with 2.0's hand. He leapt sideways, dodging 2.0's fingers before darting forward to jab the hand with his beak.

'Hurry up, Esha,' squeaked Broccoli. 'We've got to help him!'

I wriggled the second Gecko Glove on to my other hand and placed it on the wall above me. **SQUELCH**. This time, I heaved myself out of the liquid, my legs sliding free with a loud **SHLURP**. I unstuck the right glove and reached above my head, lifting myself a little higher.

SQUELCH by slow **SQUELCH**, I inched myself

upwards. Every single one of my muscles was on fire and I was absolutely sure that my arms were about to p^{o}p out of their sockets. But the top of the fishbowl was only a short distance away now.

Berty poked his head out of the Transporter and blinked at me. Then he stuck out his long, slobbery tongue and licked my face. I nodded and gritted my teeth. 'You're right, Berty. We can do this.'

With a final, **genius-level** push, I reached towards the top of the bowl and – **SQUELCH–SQUELCH** – dragged myself on to the edge where I sat like a ~~puffer~~ puffed-out fish, my arms and legs shaking.

2.0's eyes flashed at us through the window.

Holding tightly on to the edge of the bowl, I threw the gloves to Broccoli. His legs scrabbled against the wall as he tried to climb up. As his foot slid against the bowl, an object tumbled out of his pocket.

'NO!' shrieked Broccoli, lunging towards it. His gloved fingers brushed the air as the object KERZOOMED down and – SHLOP – disappeared into the liquid.

Archibald grinned in wicked delight.

'NOT THE MASTER GUIDE TOO!' wailed Broccoli.

'SQUAWK!' Glancing over my shoulder, I saw the hand charge at Monsieur Crépeau. He dodged clumsily sideways, lost his balance and wobbled off the control panel on to the floor. The hand scuttled back to the switches. A long antenna-like device whirred out of it and plugged itself into the control panel.

'DOOR OVERRIDE IN PROGRESS,' said the automated voice.

'Forget the guide!' I hissed, turning back towards Broccoli. 'We have to go!'

'But—'

'MOVE, BROCCOLI!'

Broccoli took one last look at the book, then he reached up with the right glove – SQUELCH – which hit the glass and – slid right off.

'What are you doing, Broccoli?' I snapped.

'The glove isn't working!' he shrieked, dangling one-handed

against the side of the bowl. 'This is what happened with the third prototype. It's **JAMMED!**'

'Jammed? Don't be ridiculous. These are the fourth prototype and they are absolutely resistant to all kinds of—'

'ESHA!' cried Broccoli as the left glove slipped down, dragging him down a little.

Honestly.

A **genius inventor** has to do absolutely everything.

'Reach for my hand,' I said, leaning down towards him.

Broccoli hesitated. 'Is that really a good—'

'DOOR OVERRIDE IN PROGRESS.'

'<u>NOW</u>, BROCCOLI!' I yelled.

Throwing the glove off his right hand, he stretched up towards me.

'DOOR OVERRIDE GRANTED.'

'GET OUT OF SIGHT, MONSIEUR CRÉPEAU!' I shouted as I pulled Broccoli on to the edge of the bowl. With a dizzy SQUAWK, he squeezed himself behind the control panel.

'PULSE TWO IN THREE MINUTES.'

A heart-dropping **CLUNK CLUNK** echoed around us as 2.0 marched inside. He picked up his hand and clicked it back on to his arm. His green eyes flashed as they scanned the room. I *held my breath* and tried to make myself as still as possible. Maybe if we were very quiet and very lucky, 2.0 might not see . . .

'Targets spotted,' said 2.0 in his low metallic thrum.

Well, it was worth a try.

'SQUAWK! SQUAWK!'

I GOGGLED as Monsieur Crépeau suddenly appeared from his hiding place.

'SQUAWK! SQUAWK!'

2.0's ears spun, his whole body **clanking** as he turned round.

'Target spotted,' he said.

'SQUAWK!' said Monsieur Crépeau. His eyes locked on to mine, his face set in a look I recognized all too well. It was the look of someone who had just had a spark of SPINGLY-TINGLY inspiration. The look of someone with an idea. He pointed his beak frantically down towards his foot. No, not his foot, I realized as I watched him – **the pet tracker.** And suddenly I knew. Even though I couldn't understand pigeon, even though I hadn't thought it possible for Monsieur Crépeau to have a SPINGLY-TINGLY idea, I knew exactly what he wanted us to do.

'Are you sure?' I yelled.

Monsieur Crépeau nodded, then he flapped his wings, puffed out his chest and waddled away from 2.0. 'SQUAWK! SQUAWK!'

2.0 blinked at Monsieur Crépeau, then strode after him.

'WHAT IS MONSIEUR CRÉPEAU DOING?' shouted Broccoli.

'Buying us time to ESCAPE!'

'WE HAVE TO HELP HIM!'

'WE CAN'T! NOT RIGHT NOW! WE'LL FIND HIM ONCE WE'VE GOT THE MOLECULAR MODULATOR!'

I glanced *wildly* around the room. The door was too far away, but there had to be something else – another door or window or . . .

As I looked up, my eye fell on the CLOUD EXTRACTOR.

WAIT JUST A MOMENT.

A single, zinging spark suddenly LIT UP my brain. cells.

'I've got it!' I yelled. I pointed to the
CLOUD EXTRACTOR. 'We're going to

'PULSE TWO IN ONE MINUTE.'
PUT-PUT-PUT!

Glancing over my shoulder, I saw
a string of pigeon pellets *TORPEDO* out of
Monsieur Crépeau's rear and . . . miss 2.0 completely. In one
swift movement, the robot grabbed hold of Monsieur Crépeau,
slipped him inside his metal flap and turned back towards
us. He moved quickly, his whole body crashing through the
fishbowls and ropes as he came forward.

'**RUN!**' I yelled.

We leapt off the bowl and *sprinted* along the ropes.

'PULSE TWO INITIATED.'

BOOM!

I braced myself as the wave rippled across the room. Hundreds of clouds rose up from the fishbowls around us.

CLUNK CLUNK.

'NOW!' I yelled.

'WAAAAAAAGH!' shrieked Broccoli as he jumped clumsily off the rope and bounced directly on to a cloud. Archibald poked his head out, his face shining in glee as he looked around.

CLUNK CLUNK.

Out of the corner of my eye, I saw 2.0's hand reach out towards me, his metallic fingers so close I could smell the polish and oil.

With a jump that would have impressed a cricket, I *leapt* off the rope . . .

down . . . down . . . down . . .

SHLOP!

I landed on top of a cloud.

A slightly damp, raspberry-smelling cloud.

Up I floated . . .

the mouth of the cloud extractor

growing bigger and **bigger** . . .

the fishbowls growing further and further away.

Glancing up, I saw Broccoli looking down at me, his nose twitching in *panic.*

'WHERE DOES THIS THING G—'

But I didn't hear any more because he

disappeared into the cloud extractor,

snot and all.

CLUNK CLUNK.

Looking down, I saw 2.0's head move upwards. His green eyes blinked rapidly as they met mine, then he reached up towards me. I held my breath as his arm shot out further and further, almost-probably certain that I was about to be robo-napped YET AGAIN when . . .

BER-CHING! ←

His arm juddered to a stop a few centimetres below me. I grinned.

Ernie might have given 2.0 detachable parts, but he hadn't thought to fit him with extra-extendable arms (this is yet another reason why he is **NOT** a **genius** like me).

'You won't get us this time, tin-head!' I shouted. Berty peered out of the Transporter, his tail quivering. 'We'll find you, Monsieur Crépeau!' I shouted, hoping he could hear me. 'Everything is under controoooool!'

Broccoli has just pointed out that you, the Reader, may need a moment to recover from **ALL** the excitement of the previous pages. He has also said that he would have liked such a moment, but he did not get the chance because he was floating on top of a cloud.

I have reminded him that being a **genius inventor's apprentice** means being ready for adventure AT ALL TIMES (Clause 234 of the Apprentice–Inventor Agreement). This may or may not include cloud surfing, shrinking, and other undisclosed activities.

[A note from Broccoli: I'm quite certain there are only 200 clauses in the Apprentice-Inventor Agreement.]

However, I understand that you, the Reader, may **not** be used to spectacular tales of the SHRUNKEN variety so I have included an empty space below to help you catch a breath.

Empty space to catch a breath.
(no movement required).

The <u>New-and-Improved</u> Plan

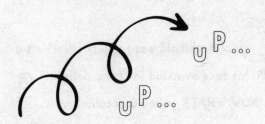

U P...

U P ...

U P I went ...

into the **enormous** mouth of the extractor.
The clouds gleamed softly, shining a soft
purple light across the metal walls.

WHIRRRRRRR-BRRRRRRRR!

'LOOK!' shouted Broccoli, his snot jiggling as he
pointed above us.

Glancing up, I saw that there was an enormous fan fixed
to the end of the extractor pipe. One by one, the clouds
floated towards it and swished away like bubbles in the wind.

WHIRRRRRRR-BRRRRRRRR!

UH-OH.

If we stayed on the clouds, we'd either:

① Get chopped up by the fan blades (TERRIBLE).

OR

② Fall back down again (DISASTROUS).

Archibald was happily munching a cloudy tuft, his face wrinkled in fizzy delight.

'NOW WHAT?' yelled Broccoli.

'There!' I shouted. A short distance below the fan, the extractor narrowed, another vent opening on its right. 'We have to jump!'

Broccoli nodded in grim determination, his nose dripping.

WHIRRRRRRR-BRRRRRRRR!

Berty poked his head out of the Transporter and whined.

WHIRRRRRRR-BRRRRRRRR!

With a loud whimper, my sniffly apprentice swept up his cloud-chomping tortoise and threw himself towards the vent, landing with a painful **BANG.**

I flinched.

'OW,' groaned Broccoli.

'You ready, Berty?' I said as we neared the vent. He squealed and dived back inside the Transporter.

'Three, two, ONE –' I *leapt* off the cloud and tumbled awkwardly on to the metal.

'Well –' I stood up, smoothed out my dungarees and pulled out the map that Meteorologist Brenda had given us. 'That turned out *better than I expected*.'

'Better than –' spluttered Broccoli. His snot dropped a centimetre as he checked his watch. '2.0 has Monsieur Crépeau. We've only got **one hour** to big ourselves and we've still got three floors left between us and the Big-o-Meter.' He stopped with a sorry sniff and held Archibald up to his face. 'And I've lost the *Tortoise Inspections Master Guide*. This mission has just gone from **bad** to

THE WORST.'

'There's Lift X,' I murmured to myself, checking the map. I pulled the Earscope out of my Inventor's Kit (adapted from Uncle Binny's stethoscope), wiped the metal end and placed it against the bottom of the vent.

'Esha, are you listening to me?' said Broccoli.

'Course I'm listening,' I snorted. A sequence of peculiar gurgling noises echoed through the earplugs.

(OK, so maybe I wasn't 100% listening to Broccoli, but it is very hard to pay attention to a flappy apprentice when you are working out the next step of an important mission.)

[A note from Broccoli: I was not flappy.]

'None of this was part of the plan!' he said, staring into the gloom of the vent ahead of us. 'How are we going to get to Lift X now?'

'You really must learn to stop worrying, Broccoli,' I said, swivelling the Earscope dial to **METAL**. Suddenly the gurgling noise

transformed into different sounds – I could hear the cloud machine, the **CLUNK CLUNK** of 2.0, the door opening and closing. 'Chapter 48 of the *Inventor's Handbook* says that a **genius inventor** must be able to devise new-and-improved plans for any and all situations,' I continued. 'We escaped a Guzzler, remember? That makes us experts at new-and-improved plans.' I waved the Earscope at him. 'We can use this to **hear** what's in the rooms below us.'

'So?'

'So we might not have the Go-Glider, but we can use the

Earscope to hear our way through the vents to Lift X. I knew it would come in handy for something more than spying on Nishi.'

'What about Monsieur Crépeau? Even if we big ourselves and get the molecular modulator, we need to find him to change him back.'

I pulled out the pet-tracker console. 'I put a tracker on him, remem— Ah.' There was a (teensy-tiny) crack running along the console. 'Must've landed on it.'

"You broke it?" said Broccoli shrilly.

'Don't be ridiculous, Broccoli. It's just a small crack.' I switched the console on. The screen spluttered to life. 'See?' I said, grinning triumphantly. 'Perfectly functional. Using my genius pet-tracker technology, we should be able to see exactly where he is . . .' The screen flashed a fuzzy grey then blinked at me.

I shook the console and waved it in the air in front of me. 'Must be these vents,' I muttered. 'They're stopping the signal from getting through.'

'Or it's broken,' said Broccoli sourly.

'It's not broken,' I snapped, slipping the tracker console into my pocket. 'It just needs time to pick up a signal.'

I switched on my Inventor's Torch and marched past him into the vent. 'Now are you coming or not?'

And so, dear Reader, we began . . .

. . . my torch throwing strange *shadows* around us . . .

as we (bravely) journeyed forward . . .

our shoes

**thump-
thumping**

across the metal . . .

We hadn't gone far when the vent split into two different directions. Choosing the one on the left, I kneeled down and placed the Earscope's end against the metal. The loud ticking of clocks filled my ears as I moved along the vent.

TICK-TOCK!

TOCK-TICK!

TICK-TOCK!

'Clocks,' I said, checking the map. 'Lots and lots of — here! We must be above The Clock Nest. See? And there's Lift X on the end. It's this way. Come on!'

Long tongues of rust gleamed either side of us as we hurried onwards.

'I don't like this,' said Broccoli behind me. 'And I **hate** being this small.'

I pretended not to hear him.

'Look at you, Archie. What will the T.W.S. say? Granny Bertha will be so disappointed if I fail this inspection. She's had Archimedes ever since he was a baby. "Take good care of this one" – that's what she said to me when she brought you. And look what's happened.'

Archibald rolled his eyes and snickered rudely as if to say, 'grow a shell, human'.

Fortunately, I was rescued from Broccoli's whinging by the pet tracker, which whirred to life at that moment.

[A note from Broccoli: I was most definitely not whinging.]

I pulled it out of my pocket and peered at the screen.

'Look, Broccoli!' I exclaimed, my inventor's instincts tingling with excitement. 'Do you see that dot?' I pointed at the tracker. 'That's Monsieur Crépeau.' I checked the map. 'He's on the third floor. In Professor Rathbone's laboratory. I told you the tracker was still working.'

'Hurry up!' said a man's voice impatiently. 'That TV crew is going to be here within the hour and they're expecting another of my Rathbone marvels! Now, where were we, Ernie?'

The tracker crackled.

'That must be Ernie's uncle. Come on!' I hissed, slapping the side.

'– human-animal transformation – you would need a molecular modulator – in the Postal Room – on loan –

out of bounds—'

I *groaned*. Part of me had almost been hoping that Ernie's uncle wouldn't be able to help him.

'How does it work?' echoed Ernie's voice.

Broccoli sneezed.

'Can I see it?'

'– not now – far **more important work** – teething problems in the Weather Simulation Room – *delicate business* – can't risk a malfunction on **live TV**–'

'But—'

Suddenly his uncle's voice buzzed through the tracker, loud and clear.

'I've been more than patient with your *little gismos*, Ernie, but today is **important**. One *wrong* measurement with the Weather Simulation Room and we could have a weathernova on our hands – could swallow the *entire planet*—'

'THE *ENTIRE*

PLANET?'

squeaked Broccoli,

his face turning pale.

'They're *not gismos*, Uncle Rathbone.' Ernie's voice sounded strangely flat.

'This is *real* inventing, do you understand? None of your tinkering.'

For one teensy-tiny moment, I understood how Rat-Bone must be feeling. He might have been my **ARCH-NEMESIS** and he was absolutely NOT as **genius** as me, but I knew how **ANNOYING** it was when your family didn't understand your **inventing brilliance**.

'And get your robot out of here. Last time, he left an oil patch on the floor—'

Suddenly the tracker cut out again. I waved it around in the air, but it stayed silent, the screen blank.

'He knows,' said Broccoli. He swallowed and looked at me, his snot quivering. 'Ernie knows about the molecular modulator.'

'Then we have to move faster,' I said, already speeding ahead. 'Even if Rat-Bone gets the molecular modulator, he still needs the RoarEasy, remember? He can't change Monsieur Crépeau back without it. Stop looking so worried, Broccoli. This is just a minor—'

The tracker buzzed again.

'– escaped?' echoed Ernie. The tracker was *whirring* **so loudly** that I could hardly hear what he was saying. 'What do you mean – *they escaped?*'

The screen flickered again, Ernie's voice exp**lod**ing around the vent before the tracker cut out completely.

'FIND them, 2.0!'

SPI-DROIDS

We hurried along the vent, our footsteps echoing loudly in the gloom.

Broccoli sniffed miserably behind me.

A short distance ahead, the vent split again, continuing straight and left. The clang of bells echoed through the Earscope as I checked the one ahead of us. 'The Bell Cavity,' I said, examining the map. 'Lift X is that way. Shouldn't be much—' Suddenly my torch flickered, plunging us into **TOTAL, toe-curling, DARKNESS.** Berty whined. I gave it a shake. The torch sputtered back on again with a shrill **beeping** noise.

'That's the low-battery warning,' I muttered. 'Broccoli, give me the spares.'

He blinked at me. 'What spares?'

'The spare batteries, Broccoli,' I said impatiently. 'Do you hear that beeping noise? That means we only have ten minutes until the torch runs out completely.'

 'I don't have the spares.'

'What do you mean?'

He sniffed. 'I thought *you'd* brought them.'

'Why would I have brought them?'

'Because you packed the Inventor's Kit,' retorted Broccoli.

'Carrying spare parts for our important inventions is an apprentice's job, Broccoli,' I snapped. 'Not mine.'

The torch beeped shrilly between us.

Broccoli folded his arms across his chest and sniffed. 'You should have told me. I thought you'd packed everything. That would have been the *sensible* thing to do.'

'Sensible?' I snorted, prickling with annoyance. 'You brought a tortoise-care pouch and you **forgot the spare batteries?**'

Broccoli flushed. 'I didn't forget.'

'This wouldn't have happened if you hadn't been so busy flapping about that tort—'

That's when I heard it.

CLACKETY CLACKETY CLACK!

I looked into the vent to the left of us.

Something was stirring in the darkness.

Something

'What is that?' whispered Broccoli.

My inventor's instincts tingled to RED ALERT.

CLACKETY CLACKETY CLACK . . .

The noise was growing louder.

CLACKETY CLACKETY CLACK . . .

CLACKETY CLACKETY –

I breathed in sharply.

Creeping out of the gloom of the vent were *two*
**HUGE** spiders.

Only these weren't *normal* spiders.

They were

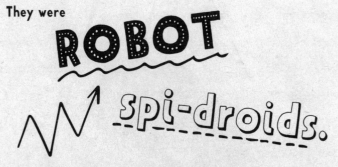

They were built entirely of polished black metal with
long, spiky legs. Their metallic heads were domed and
fitted with a pair of shiny metal pincers. But the **worst**
thing about them was their *eyes*. They were shaped
like long narrow slits and took up most of their head,
glowing red in the darkness.

Broccoli took one look at them and **EXPLODED** into a sneeze-a-thon. Berty dived behind me, his tail quivering so hard that I could feel the walls of the vent shaking. Archibald made a noise that sounded like, 'come at me, metal-brains'.

The spi-droids stared at us for a moment.

'Maybe they're friendly,' I said to Broccoli, taking a step back.

The first spi-droid moved forward, its pincers snapping together with menace.

'That doesn't look friendly to me,' whispered Broccoli.

I swallowed as I looked up at the spi-droids, my brain *whirring* with all the possible ways out of this particular situation. Fortunately, I am a **genius inventor** and I know *exactly* what to do when you are being stared down by a mysterious metal spider that is **TRIPLE** your size.

'RUN!' I shouted, sprinting into the vent ahead of us. 'WE NEED TO GET TO LIFT X!'

Broccoli didn't need to be told twice.

Our feet clanged across the metal as the spi-droids came after us, their legs skittering across the vent with a heart-dropping **CLACKETY CLACKETY.**

I glanced back over my shoulder, **GOGGLING** at their speed. Suddenly the spi-droid at the very front made a **LOUD** *whirring* noise. Its metallic head lifted a little to reveal a tiny robotic cannon.

'WHAT IS THAT?' shrieked Broccoli.

'NOTHING GOOD!' I shouted.

ZUT!

A pellet **blasted** out of the cannon and **splattered** just behind us with a stomach-turning **STICKY** sound.

ZUT!

Another pellet **EXPLODED** into the air behind us.

ZUT! ZUT!

My torch beeped shrilly, the light flickering around us.

'We're not going to be able to outrun them,' gasped Broccoli.

'But we can 𝔰𝔩𝔬𝔴 them down!' I huffed.

I stuck my hand into my Inventor's Kit and slid out the third prototype of my Slimer Shot (ingeniously adapted from a water cannon). Hoisting it over my shoulder, I aimed my glorious invention at the first spi-droid and fired.

KERPOOSH!

A slime splodge flew across the air in a magnificent **gooey burst** and hit the spi-droid between its eyes. The spi-droid froze, its body sizzling with bright blue sparks.

'It worked!' I shouted in glee. 'Broccoli, did you see—'

'ESHA, WATCH OUT!' yelled Broccoli.

My mouth dropped as the second spi-droid crawled on to the ceiling. With eye-popping acrobatics, it scuttled, *upside-down*, over its partner, its red eyes locked on us like lasers.

ZUT!

Before I could move, a pellet *rocketed* out towards the Slimer Shot. It whizzed out of my hands and stuck to the side of the vent in a sticky, spidery web.

'YOU STINKING SPIDER-HEAD,' I roared.

'WE HAVE TO MOVE!' shouted Broccoli as I tried to pull the Slimer Shot free. He yanked me out of the way as another pellet landed with a gluey GLOP a hand's width away from me.

Berty squealed in fright as we raced along the vent. The pet tracker *whirred* to life in my pocket, buzzed loudly, then cut out again.

CLACKETY CLACKETY CLACK!

'Oh no,' panted Broccoli.

A short way ahead of us, the vent split again.

'WHICH WAY?'

ZUT!

'RIGHT!' I guessed wildly. (By my **genius** calculations, we had a 50% chance of being correct and reaching Lift X. By the same calculations, I was 100% not able to use the Earscope at that particular moment.)

ZUT! ZUT!

We sprinted into the vent on the right.

'WE SHOULD'VE GONE LEFT!' yelled Broccoli, pointing ahead of him.

Not far in front of us was a large gap, then another vent. 'It's a **dead end!'**

'No, it's not!'

ZUT! ZUT!

More pellets echoed over our heads as the spi-droid scuttled closer.

CLACKETY CLACKETY CLACK!

'We're going to jump!' I puffed.

'WHAT?' shrieked Broccoli, his face shiny with sweat.

Archibald (who looked like he was having the time of his life) grinned in delight.

'Get ready!'

'ESHA, THIS IS A **BAD** IDEA!' shouted Broccoli.

Berty whined in agreement.

We were almost by the gap now, close enough for me to see that it was ever so slightly bigger than I had expected. My torch flashed again, the light wobbling wildly around the vent.

CLACKETY CLACKETY CLACK!

'A VERY BAD IDEA!' yelled Broccoli.

The end of the vent loomed in front of us.

I took a **deep** breath.

'ESHA! ARE YOU LISTEN—'

'NOW!'

With all the strength of my teensy-tiny body, I threw myself over the gap. Air whooshed past my ears as I flew across the empty space. My legs cycled wildly through a GREAT BIG NOTHING. Berty shrieked as the other vent zoomed up to meet us. For one heart-popping moment, I thought I wasn't going to make it.

My very short inventor's life flashed before my eyes . . .

then . . .

THUD!

A fiery pain jolted through my body as I landed on the other side.

THUD!

A moment later, Broccoli smacked into the vent behind me with a loud groan. The second spi-droid stopped, teetering clumsily on the opposite edge. Its head *whirred* up, its eyes fixed on me, unblinking.

'WHAT'S THE MATTER, METAL-MOUTH?' I shouted. 'TOO SCARED TO jump?'

The spi-droid scuttled back, then, with a speed that took my breath away, it raced forward and launched itself across the empty space. I stepped back, mouth dropping, as it soared across the air in one swift, splendid sweep.

We sprinted forward, the floor juddering as the spi-droid landed behind us. Berty squealed and tucked himself so deeply into the Transporter that all I could see was the trembling tip of his tail.

Along the vent we went . . .

scrambling up a grille . . .

our footsteps thud-thudding across the metal . . .

My torch beeped, the light flicking.

ZUT! ZUT!

The spi-droid **thundered** closer. I pulled
out the Pooper Scooper, set it to reverse and aimed it at
the spi-droid. A string of tiny poop pellets whizzed over
Broccoli's head and bounced off the metal.

(Well, it was worth a try.)

My torch flickered again, the beeping noise now
SHRILLER than a pigeon on a skateboard, until with
a final, sorry BEEP it died, **plunging us into
darkness.**

'I CAN'T SEE WHERE I'M GOING!' squealed Broccoli ahead
of me.

'JUST KEEP MOVING!' I panted, my legs burning from
all the pesky running.

ZUT! ZUT!

The spi-droid's eyes flickered frighteningly red behind
us. My brain whirred for a **GENIUS** plan, but it is very
hard to think of a **genius** plan when you are:

① Running from an enormous spider robot in complete **DARKNESS**.

② Sort-of-almost-definitely **LOST**.

ZUT! ZUT!

'WAIT!' shouted Broccoli. 'THAT LOOKS LIKE LIGHT AHEAD!'

'WHERE?'

ZUT! ZUT!

'I CAN'T SEE ANYTHING!'

'WATCH OUT!' squealed Broccoli somewhere in front of me. Something small and round rattled beneath my feet. 'I THINK THESE ARE PEBBLES—'

'WAAARRGGHHH!'

(So much for an **ADVANCE** warning.)

My feet flew out from under me. I slid forward, crashing into my apprentice. We spun and rolled, the **CLACKETY CLACK** of the spi-droid growing louder and louder as we zoomed along the vent and out through a giant hole . . .

~~Broccoli gets in a huff~~ A Slight Disagreement

Z**I**NG!

I shot out of the vent on to something soft and springy. I bounced . . . once, twice . . . three times, then landed with a **thump** on top of Broccoli.

'Ow,' he moaned.

'Couldn't you watch where you fell?' I muttered, pushing his elbow out of my mouth.

'Archie?' said Broccoli. There were damp patches on his sleeve where his snot had got tangled up with his clothes. He wobbled to his feet, his hair swaying like jelly, and glanced around wildly. 'There you are!' He lifted his evil tortoise to his face. 'Are you OK?'

Archibald grinned.

Berty peeped out of the Transporter and whined.

'Sorry about that, Berty,' I said, scratching the top of his head. I slid the Pooper Scooper back into the Transporter.

'Turns out that dinosaur poop has no effect on spi-droids.'

'What is this place?' murmured Broccoli, looking around.

The world spun round me as I staggered to my feet. Everywhere around us was reddish sand. It rose and fell in **enormous** dunes, each speck glittering like a tiny diamond. A sign on the wall read: THE BOTANICAL GARDENS. Under it was another sign that said:

WARNING
DON'T
FEED THE
PLANTS.

'Botanical Gardens?' said Broccoli with a wary sniff. 'This place looks more like a desert.'

ZING!

There was a loud *whirring* behind us as the spi-droid shot out of the vent. We leapt out of the way as it crashed into the sand, its pincers clicking wildly.

'SIGNAL LOST,' said an automated voice. 'SIGNAL LOST.'

Its eyes blinked at us, then it powered down with a faint beeping noise.

I stared at the spi-droid, then I leaned forward and poked one of its legs.

'Esha,' gasped Broccoli.

But the spi-droid didn't move.

'Look,' I said. On the side of its legs, etched neatly into the metal, were the words **PROPERTY OF ERNIE RATHBONE**.

'Rat-Bone,' I growled, prickling with anger. 'He must have been after the RoarEasy.'

'Heat sensors and cameras,' said Broccoli, examining the spi-droid. 'That's how he was tracking us.'

I clenched my fists. 'Wait till I get my hands on that AIR-BRAIN. He's going to pay for making me lose the Slimer Shot.'

'We need to get out of here,' said Broccoli, glancing up warily as if he expected an army of spi-droids to come whizzing out of the vent. 'If the signal was active when we landed, Ernie could be here at any moment. How far are we from the Big-o-Meter?'

I looked at the map. 'The Botanical Gardens is on –' I paused and stared at the map in surprise – 'the fourth floor.' I glanced up at the ceiling. 'The spi-droid must've chased us further up than we realized. We've got one floor left to go.' I stuck the map back into my pocket and took out the pet tracker. 'Come on,' I said, waving the console in the air, but the screen stayed blank.

'Told you it wasn't a signal problem,' said Broccoli RUDELY. 'It's broken.'

'How many times do I have to tell you, Broccoli?' I snapped. 'It's *not* broken.'

He ignored me and checked his watch, his face paling. 'We've got less than an hour to change Monsieur Crépeau before the TV crew arrive. And we've got just over thirty minutes to big ourselves. We're *never* going to make it to the fifth floor in time. Not when we're this small.' His eye fell back on the spi-droid. He stared at it for a long moment, chewing his lip thoughtfully. 'Maybe we should use that.'

'What?' I said incredulously. 'Have you forgotten that it was trying to WEB us?'

'That's when Ernie still had a signal. He doesn't now. I think – I think it would be safe to restart it.'

'You think?'

'You saw how fast it moved. If we can get it to work, we can use it to get to Lift X.'

I snorted. 'Don't be **ridiculous,** Broccoli. We don't need Rat-Bone's invention to get to the fifth floor. We can do that *ourselves*.'

Broccoli opened his mouth as if he were about to argue.

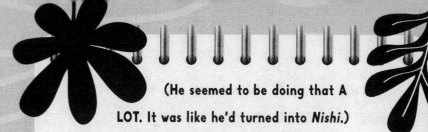

(He seemed to be doing that A
LOT. It was like he'd turned into *Nishi*.)

'Let's go,' I said, marching forward. 'And keep your
eyes open for an exit!'

Plants with long, twisted creepers rose up from the
sand around us. The creepers were a glossy plum colour
and **ENORMOUS**. Some dangled downwards like
huge cat's claws. Others poked out from under the sand
like crooked fingers. Across the vines were dark yellow
flowers, their petals tightly closed.

Berty danced forward, stopping momentarily to test the
sand with his tongue before spitting it out again.

'I don't like this place,' whispered Broccoli.

For once, I couldn't help thinking that my apprentice
was correct. My inventor's instincts had been itching like
mad ever since we'd got here, but I decided it was best not
to tell Broccoli that.

Not when he'd start **FLAPPING** even more.

[A note from Broccoli: I don't flap.]

'Can you see a way out?' he asked.

'Not yet.'

We raced through the sand . . .

200

up one dune . . . down another . . .

and still there was **NO SIGN** of a door or an exit.

'How big is this place?' I panted. 'Feels like we've been here for hours.'

(OK, so maybe it wasn't as long as that, but we were teensy-tiny and even a little bit of running felt **VERY LONG**.)

Broccoli tugged my sleeve. 'Esha, look.'

I glanced down to where he was pointing. There, on the sand, was the spi-droid, exactly where we'd left it. His snot wobbled. 'We've gone round **IN A CIRCLE!**'

I stared at the spi-droid in **confusion**, then I scratched my chin. 'Well, I don't know how **that** happened.'

Broccoli's lip wobbled, his snot dropping to **PANIC MODE**.

'We've got twenty-five minutes left to big ourselves,' he said, checking his watch. 'We just wasted **five** whole minutes.'

'Well, these plants are **HUMONGOUS**,' I snapped. 'It's not my fault if—'

'Yes it is!' interrupted Broccoli crossly. His snot wobbled. **'IT'S ALL <u>YOUR</u> FAULT!'**

I folded my arms across my chest and **glared** at him.

'And what *exactly* do you mean by THAT?' I said.

Broccoli hesitated, then he took a deep breath and looked me in the eye. 'If you hadn't brought the RoarEasy to school, Monsieur Crépeau wouldn't have turned into a pigeon.' His snot wavered as he spoke. 'We wouldn't have had to come here to change him back, we wouldn't have got shrunk and we **definitely** wouldn't be in the middle of this – this – 𝕕𝕖𝕤𝕖𝕣𝕥!'

'It's not my fault that Monsieur Crépeau changed into a pigeon,' I snapped. 'That was an accident.'

'*And* we wouldn't have ended up in the Cloud Chamber if you'd flown the Go-Glider properly,' said Broccoli sourly.

'At least I brought the Go-Glider. You didn't even remember the spare batteries for the torch,' I retorted. 'And, in case you've forgotten, you were the one who made us crash. All because you were too busy worrying about that **stupid** pouch and your **silly** tortoise!'

Broccoli flushed.

Berty whined.

Archibald made a noise that sounded like, 'now you've done it'.

'His name is Archibald,' said Broccoli fiercely.
He stroked the top of his head. 'And he's not a silly
tortoise. He's my friend. And if we fail this inspection—'

URGH.

'I DON'T CARE about the inspection!'

I exploded. 'I c𝕒r𝕖 about the mission. I c𝕒r𝕖 about
finding the molecular modulator and changing Monsieur
Crépeau back and winning the Brain Trophy. I c𝕒r𝕖
about what's IMPORTANT.'

Broccoli's nose quivered. 'The inspection *is* important,'
he said.

I snorted.

'You think you're right all the time but you're not,'
continued Broccoli. His snot trembled, his voice shaking
with indignation. 'If you hadn't brought Berty, we
wouldn't have got shrunk. I told you not to, but you
didn't listen.' He sniffed. 'You **NEVER** listen. And if
we stay shrunk forever it's going to be *your fault!*'

Archibald looked between the two of us, his eyes
growing **wider** and **wider**.

'Well, if that's how you feel, why don't you find the
Big-o-Meter yourself?' I snapped crossly.

'Maybe I will,' said Broccoli.

'Good. Then I won't have to listen to you flapping all the time.' I knotted my arms across my chest and gave him a super-charged ESHA LASER GLARE. 'I'll change Monsieur Crépeau back into a human myself. I don't need your help. In fact, I don't even need an apprentice. I only took you on because you so obviously needed someone to make your BORING life more exciting. I'm perfectly clever enough to be a genius inventor ON MY OWN.'

Broccoli breathed in sharply, his snot wobbling.

Even Archibald looked shocked, his face wrinkling in disappointment as he stared at me.

'If you say so,' said Broccoli coldly. He slung the rucksack off his shoulder and handed it to me. 'Here's the RoarEasy.

→ I quit.' ←

'Fine. In fact, double fine,' I retorted as he began walking away. 'I don't need you. You'll only slow me down.'

Berty blinked at me, his eyes round with concern.

'What are you looking at?' I snapped.

His amber eyes widened; with a soft whine he dropped his head between his legs.

I sighed.

'Sorry, Berty,' I said. 'This isn't your fault.' I looked back at my snivelly ~~apprentice~~ ex-apprentice, who had bent down beside Ernie's spi-droid.

A peculiar sensation prickled the corners of my eyes.

'This sand is getting everywhere,' I mumbled, turning round. For half a moment, I expected Broccoli to realize that he'd made a terrible mistake and come after me. But my ~~apprentice~~ ex-apprentice stayed beside the spi-droid.

Berty touched his head against my hand.

'You're right, Berty,' I declared. 'I'm a **genius inventor**. I don't need Broccoli.' I marched through the sand, absolutely *not* thinking about all the cool inventions we had created together. 'Come on. We have an exit to find.'

This time, I took a different direction through the sand, Berty bounding along after me. After a few seconds, he stopped and looked over his shoulder as if he were waiting for Broccoli.

'In fact, I don't know why anyone would want an apprentice,' I continued. 'They just **sneeze** and they're scared of everything. Sure, they're useful for listening to your important ideas and carrying stuff, *especially* when you've got a Transporter and a rucksack, but—'

Suddenly there was a **loud click** above us like a switch being turned off. **'SLEEP MODE DEACTIVATED,'** said an automated voice. The lights dimmed into a dark-blue glow. I licked my lips and looked around at the twisty-wisty creepers around us. Strangely, they looked **even bigger** than they had before. Berty whimpered and pressed his head against my leg.

'It's OK, Berty,' I said. 'There's nothing to be afraid—'

I froze. Out of the corner of my eye, I'd seen something. In fact, *seen* wasn't the right word. I'd felt something. A movement in the air. A tiny flicker. Without moving my head, I glanced sideways.

Nothing.

The plants were still and silent, exactly as they had— *Wait.* I stepped forward and eyed the plant in front of me, my inventor's instincts twitching to **RED ALERT.** The flower in front of me was now open, its petals curling outwards like **giant tongues.** At its centre was a shimmery violet shoot. I peered closer. Around the centre of the flower were sharp pointed things that looked exactly like . . .

TEETH.

'Broc—' I began, then remembered that I didn't have an apprentice any more. 'Berty,' I whispered, 'are you seeing what I'm seeing?'

He blinked back at me, then he started licking himself.

I sighed. Not having an apprentice was going to be trickier than I'd thought.

At that moment, the pet tracker whirred to life.

'There it is, 2.0!' buzzed Ernie's voice.

A loud WHOOSHING noise ripped through the air as one of the plant's creepers rocketed towards me. With a grasshopper-level leap, I dived out of the way, the Transporter flying out of my hands. The creeper swiped empty sand. Berty looked up, his eyes widening as he caught sight of the plant.

'The molecular modulator – we've got it!' said Ernie, his voice tinny through the tracker.

The creeper snapped back into the air. I watched in *horrified fascination* as it twisted back and forth like an insect's antenna. I flicked the console switch to **OFF**, but it continued to buzz loudly.

(OK, so maybe it was just a teensy-tiny bit broken.)

'Now we just have to find Esha's **stupid invention** before the TV crew arrive!'

'SQUAWK!' echoed Monsieur Crépeau's voice worriedly through the tracker before it cut out again.

With a loud shriek, Berty dived into the Transporter.

Honestly.

What T-rex was **afraid** of plants?

Before I could reach into my Inventor's Kit, the creeper came at me again, zipping through the air with a ferocity that would have been quite impressive had I not been trying to escape ATTACK BY PLANT.

I leapt backwards, the creeper **just missing me** as

it slapped against the ground. Shoving the pet tracker into my pocket, I grabbed hold of the Transporter and sprinted back in the opposite direction, Berty shrieking wildly.

The creeper came at me **again.**

I flung myself sideways, the Transporter whizzing out of my hands for a second time. Berty tumbled out of it, bounced across the sand and *somehow* landed on his feet.

'Run, Berty!' I shouted, waving my arms at him. He hesitated, his amber eyes watching me in confusion. 'GO ON. RUN! I'M RIGHT BEHIND YOU!'

With a frightened squeal, he darted off across the sand. One by one, the plants around me were waking up. Their flower petals curled outwards, creepers slithering across the ground with a LOUD HISS. The sand shivered and shook as a few of them wriggled up to the surface. I slid and stumbled as I tried to outrun them, but it is very difficult to outrun anything when you are SPRINTING ON SHIFTING SAND.

A thunderous hiss EXPLODED close behind me as a creeper lunged forward and wrapped round my foot.

'LET ME GO!' I screamed. Air rushed past my face, the ground moving away **AT ROCKET SPEED**. The rucksack (with the RoarEasy **INSIDE** it) tumbled down to the sand along with (double sigh) **ALL** the remaining items from my Inventor's Kit, including:

1. My last reserve apple
2. The Earscope
3. A pencil sharpener
4. Two juggling balls
5. A packet of tissues
6. A twisted pan handle
7. Five seashells
8. Two pairs of rainbow shoelaces
9. A roll of foil
10. One pack of pumpkin seeds
11. Cotton buds
12. A ball of rubber bands
13. One magnifying glass
14. Two whistles
15. My Inventor's Torch
16. Birdseed

and **SO ON.**

EUGH.

Not AGAIN.

~~[A note from Broccoli: I did warn Esha that she shouldn't keep her Inventor's Kit in her dungarees. Especially after what happened with the worms last time.]~~

The creeper pulled me up, higher and higher, so high that in the distance I spotted a door that read: EXIT. But, of course, that was absolutely **ZERO** help to me at that particular moment.

'DID YOU HEAR WHAT I SAID?' I yelled. 'LET GO OF ME, PLANT-FACE!'

The plant hissed with glee, its enormous flower mouth opening wide to

and all I could think about was how unfair it was that I should survive a **T-rex** and a Guzzler only to be eaten by a PONCY PLANT – when another creeper lashed out towards me. It curled itself round my other foot and **RUDELY** pulled me in the opposite direction.

The plants hissed at each other as they
pulled me

left –   right . . .

                        right –

left . . .

                        the floor and ceiling wobbling so
fast that I was sure I was about to be sick.

And now, dear Reader, you must be thinking that this
was **THE END** of my inventing chronicles (again), but you
would be quite **WRONG**. Because I am a **genius inventor**
and even as I was spinning through the air,
my brain was *whirring* for a way out.

It took me exactly 1.5 seconds to realize
that I couldn't think of any ideas.

Not when I was stuck in the middle of this vile
vegetation.

Not when I was so dizzy that I couldn't think **STRAIGHT**.

That only left me with one option.

I took a deep breath in preparation. Then . . .

'**HEEEEEELLLLLPP!**' I BELLOWED at the top of my voice.

'BROCCOLI, HELP ME!'

Meanwhile . . .
[written mostly by Broccoli]

I inspected the spi-droid in sniffly silence. Archibald looked up at me with a worried look on his face.

'I'm fine, thank you, Archie,' I said.

I checked the spi-droid's legs and body, but there was no sign of a control panel. Holding carefully on to Archibald, I climbed on top of the spi-droid, perching awkwardly on the metal behind its head.

Esha was wrong. We might have invented the RoarEasy together, but it was *her fault* that Monsieur Crépeau had turned into a pigeon. If she hadn't brought our invention to school, none of this would have happened.

[A note from Esha: I have reminded Broccoli that accidents are part of inventing. I am not quite sure why he forgot about this and decided to be so UNREASONABLE.]

After a minute, I found what I was looking for. Cleverly hidden behind the spi-droid's head was a metal flap, already half open, with a complex network of wires and receivers inside. 'There's the control panel, Archie! It must have popped open when the spi-droid fell.'

I pushed the flap wide and peered inside.

Archibald watched me in gloomy silence.

'Don't look at me like that,' I said. 'I don't want to be Esha's apprentice any more, OK? She never listens to me. It's her fault we got shrunk in the first place. If she'd kept hold of Berty, we'd still be the right size.' I sniffed. 'Ernie's spi-droid is our best chance of making it to the Big-o-Meter in time.' I sneezed. 'Or we'll stay this tiny forever and the Tortoise Welfare Society will take you away.'

Archibald continued to stare at me, his face wrinkled in the same sad expression he had whenever we said goodbye to Granny Bertha and Archimedes.

I pretended not to notice.

'Here it is. You see, Archie?' I pointed at the receiver built into the control panel. Beside it was a label that read REMOTE CONTROL. 'Ernie must have been using a transmitter to control it.' I peered more closely at the receiver. Underneath it was another switch labelled VOICE CONTROL. 'He must have built that in as a back-up,' I said, impressed.

[A note from Esha: I am not sure why Broccoli was impressed. Even a peanut brain would have installed a secondary control function. It's *basic* inventing.]

bigger than Ernie's brain

I moved my hand towards the switch, then hesitated, my fingers hovering above it.

Archibald touched his nose to my palm.

'You're right, Archie. Ernie's not controlling it any more. It's going to be fine.'

I swallowed, took a deep breath, then flicked the switch.

For a moment, nothing happened.

Then, with a heart-stopping WHIRR, the spi-droid stirred to life. I sneezed, clinging tightly to its metal body as it rose on its long metal legs.

'VOICE CONTROL ENGAGED. STATE YOUR COMMAND.'

'Uh - I . . .' I looked at Archie, who blinked at me worriedly. 'Move forward, please,' I gabbled.

'VOICEPRINT NOT RECOGNIZED. TRY AGAIN.'

'Move forward, please,' I said again, slowly this time.

'VOICEPRINT NOT RECOGNIZED. TRY AGAIN.'

'Forward,' I said for a third time.

'VOICEPRINT NOT RECOGNIZED. TRY–'

'Again - I got it,' I said, peering inside the control panel. 'There must be a way to override–'

That's when the lights changed.

'SLEEP MODE DEACTIVATED,' said an automated voice.

I glanced up. The sand was now shadowed in a menacing blue glow. All around us, I could feel the plants moving. A loud hiss rang through the air as the flower petals opened, the creepers wriggling to life. Suddenly one of the vines lunged across the ground, curled itself round an insect-shaped body hidden in the sand and whipped it back towards a flower.

CRUNCH, CRUNCH!

I winced as it disappeared.

Archibald shot back into his shell, trembling.

[A note from Esha: I am quite sure he had the giggles.]

'I knew there was something wrong about this place,' I whispered. 'I could feel it in my nose.' A few creepers shot out of the sand behind us, slithering into the air like snakes. The hiss around me was growing louder by the second. My nose twitched. If the plants detected us, we'd be chomped . . . *again*. I couldn't let that happen. I *wouldn't*. Not this time. My fingers trembled as they moved across the wires and switches.

The spi-droid's eyes flashed as I slid the final wire into place and flicked the switch. 'VOICEPRINT OVERRIDE. STATE YOUR COMMAND.'

'Yes!' I grinned. 'It worked, Archie! It really . . .' A vicious hiss burst through the air. The plants shifted towards

us, the creepers sliding in our direction.

'Forward!' I squeaked.

'COMMAND ACCEPTED.'

The spi-droid lifted its legs and skittered clumsily across the sand.

The creepers were moving even quicker now.

'FASTER!' I shrieked.

'COMMAND ACCEPTED. ENGAGE SPEED MODE?'

One of the creepers, slightly ahead of the others, zipped out towards us.

'YES!'

With a loud whirr, the spi-droid scuttled out of reach of the creeper, which writhed in the sand, hissing angrily.

Archibald peered out of his shell.

'We have to find Esha!' I said, clutching tightly to the spi-droid. I might have quit as her apprentice but I still couldn't leave her in the gardens. Not when she might bump into a people-eating plant. Just the thought of her being eaten by a carnivorous creeper made me feel cold all over.

'ESHA!' I shouted, the spi-droid whirring across the empty stretch of sand. 'ESHA, WE HAVE TO GET OUT OF HERE! THESE PLANTS ARE . . .'

Just then, I spotted a tiny speck of movement coming across the sand towards me.

'Esha?' I said hopefully. As I watched, the speck became a blob and the blob transformed into the unmistakeable shape of a tiny T-rex.

'Albertus?' I said. He was moving with jaw-dropping speed, his feet hardly touching the ground as he flew across the sand.

'I can't see Esha,' I murmured, my stomach turning. 'You don't think—'

Archie touched a claw to my hand.

Berty was closer now, close enough for me to see his amber eyes, wide with fright. At the sight of the spi-droid, he froze, his mouth opening in a terrified . . .

'ROAR!'

'It's OK, Berty!' I shouted, waving to him. 'It's me! Broccoli!'

At that moment, a thunderous noise erupted in the distance.

'BROCCOLI, HELP ME! HEEEEEELLLLLP!'

'Esha?' A burst of relief flooded through me. 'She hasn't been eaten!'

[A note from Esha: I have reminded Broccoli that I am a **genius inventor** and I wouldn't be eaten that easily.]

Berty motioned his head towards the sound of Esha's voice, then he sprinted back in the direction he'd come, roaring loudly.

'Hang on, Berty!' I shouted, starting after him. 'I'm coming!'

The Grand Getaway
(sort of)

'**HEEEELLLPP!**' I screamed again. The creepers hissed as they pulled me one way, then the other. '**BROCCOLI! BERTY!** *ANYONE!*' ⬅

(OK, I am sure that you, the Reader, must be wondering why I didn't invent anything to get me away from these pestilent plants, but it is very hard to think of inventing when you are about to be SNAP-CRACKED at any moment.)

'**HEEEELLLPP!**'

'**ESHA!**'

From my upside-down hang-tangle, I spotted Berty racing towards me, a familiar orange-topped dot speeding behind him. My mouth dropped. My sniffly ~~apprentice~~ ex-apprentice was charging forward on Rat-Bone's spi-droid, a smirking Archibald bouncing along beside him.

'**BROCCOLI!**' I yelled. I had never been *so* happy to see him in **ALL MY GENIUS** LIFE. '**WHAT TOOK YOU SO LONG?**'

[A note from Broccoli: There is no winning with some people.]

'ESHA, THESE PLANTS ARE CARNIVOROUS!' he shouted. 'WITH TEETH!'

'YOU THINK?'

A venomous hiss erupted into the air as the plants sensed Broccoli below. One by one, they turned in his direction, the creepers quivering in anticipation. Suddenly one lunged towards the spi-droid. Berty squealed and dived out of the way.

'LEFT!' shrieked Broccoli. With LIGHTNING-FAST speed, the spi-droid scuttled out of the creeper's path. Clouds of sand ERUPTED into the air as more vines shot towards him.

'RIGHT! LEFT! THERE ARE TOO MANY!' he shrieked.

'USE THE CANNON!' I bellowed.

Broccoli's face brightened as he understood my GENIUS idea.

'FIRE, SPI-DROID!' he shouted.

'COMMAND NOT RECOGNIZED. PLEASE TRY AGAIN.'

'SHOOT!'

'COMMAND NOT RECOGNIZED. PLEASE TRY AGAIN.'

Another creeper shot out of the ground and lunged towards him with a hungry hiss.

'RIGHT! CANNON!' gabbled Broccoli, clutching tightly to the spi-droid as it dodged out of the way. 'SPIDERWEB! ROBOT WEB! WEB—'

'WEB CANNON. ENGAGE?'

'YES! ENGAGE!'

ZUT!

A pellet of sensational stickiness launched into the air, striking a creeper with a perfect **SPLAT**. It withdrew, wriggling in the air with an *angry hiss*.

ZUT! ZUT! ZUT!

A second pellet hit the creeper holding my left leg. It flinched and released its grip. My stomach spun as I lurched through the air, the ground rising up to meet me as I swung, UPSIDE DOWN, like the pendulum on a clock.

'GET THE ROAREASY!' I yelled. 'IT'S OVER THERE!'

sticky splats

'I'M A LITTLE BUSY!' shouted Broccoli, clutching on to the spi-droid as it fired another round of sticky **SPLATS**.

'BERTY! GET THE ROAREASY!' I shouted, waving at the rucksack on the sand.

He hesitated for a moment, then shot forward. He moved like a **REPTILIAN ROCKET**, his legs powering him between the creepers, until, with a loud roar, he threw himself towards the Transporter.

'NO, NOT THAT, BERTY!' I shouted.
'THE ROAREASY! IT'S IN THE RUCKSACK!'

He sprinted back towards Broccoli, the  Transporter (complete with the Pooper Scooper) bouncing in his mouth. I groaned.

'HOLD ON, ESHA!' shouted Broccoli. He hauled Berty and the Transporter on to the spi-droid. 'I'M COMING!'

'WHAT DOES IT LOOK LIKE I'M DOING?' I snapped.

ZUT!

Another pellet smacked the creeper holding my right foot. It snapped back in shock, its stem shaking dizzily.

'HA!' I shouted. 'TAKE THAT, YOU CARNIVOROUS CREEP—

AAAARRGGGHHH!'

Down I went as the creeper let go of me – down, down, down, until I landed with a **TH**_U_**MP** in an explosion of sand. Leaping to my feet (and spitting out all the itty-bitty sand I'd just swallowed), I sprinted towards the rucksack.

ZUT! ZUT!

Another creeper zoomed down towards me. I slid out of its way, ducked under another and threw myself towards the rucksack.

(A PLUS about being teensy-tiny: it is easier to DODGE things. Well . . . most of the time.)

'GOTCHA!' I yelled as my fingers clamped round the straps.

Out of the corner of my eye, I spotted a creeper WHIZZ out of the sand towards me.

ZUT!

A spurt of sticky webs BLASTED it to the side.

'Come on, Esha!' shouted Broccoli, his arm outstretched as he skittered across the sand towards me. I leapt up and grabbed hold of his hand, scrabbling on to the spi-droid.

ZUT! ZUT!

The creepers hissed, their long, thick stems sliding towards us.

'FORWARD!' shouted Broccoli.

ZUT! ZUT!

'THE EXIT IS THAT WAY!' I shouted as we sped across the sand.

ZUT! ZUT!

The spi-droid scuttled between the creepers with jaw-dropping speed. Berty whined and nestled his head into my shoulder as we bounced forward.

'THERE IT IS!' I yelled, pointing ahead. A short distance beyond the creepers was a stretch of empty sand and beyond that, towering high above our teensy-tiny heads, was a green door with the word EXIT glittering above it.

'WEB CANNON ALMOST EMPTY. PLEASE REFILL.'

'Oh no,' whispered Broccoli, his face paling.

ZUT! ZUT!

Archibald snickered gleefully.

'WEB CANNON ALMOST EMPTY. PLEASE REFILL.'

According to my genius calculations, there was probably one human step left between us and the empty stretch of sand. Unfortunately, one human step was quite LARGE when you were shrunk.

ZUT! ZUT! ZU–

With a loud splutter, the web cannon shot a last spurt of liquid and powered down.

'WEB CANNON EMPTY. PLEASE REFILL—'

'Uh – BROCCOLI?' I shouted, my inventor's instincts prickling as the spi-droid scuttled across the sand, completely and utterly EXPOSED. 'CAN'T THIS THING GO ANY FASTER?'

Before Broccoli could reply, one creeper, thinner and quicker than the rest, whizzed out towards us.

It hit the spi-droid with **such force** that we

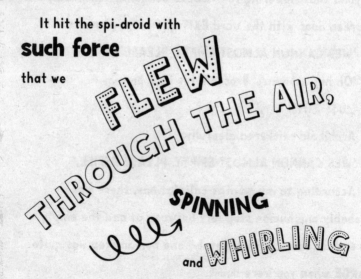

FLEW THROUGH THE AIR, SPINNING and WHIRLING

ROUND
and
ROUND until we landed with a **THUMP.**

'Move, Broccoli!' I shouted, dragging him out of the sand. Behind us, the spi-droid beeped sadly as a creeper snatched it up, its metallic body disappearing with a loud **CRUNCH.** 'The exit isn't far!'

Another creeper lunged towards us as we sprinted forward, so close that I could hear its horrible hissing growing louder and louder . . .

Archibald's head bounced up and down in delight.

The door was only a few steps ahead of us now. Glancing over my shoulder, I saw the creeper still slithering towards us.

'HOW LONG IS THIS THING?' I shouted.

'Almost there,' panted Broccoli.

We dived for the bottom of the door.

Dropping flat on to our stomachs, we crawled through

the gap, a heart-stopping hiss trailing over our shoulders.
A moment later, the creeper came under the door after

us. I crawled out the
other end and leapt to
my feet, yanking Broccoli out of the way as it lunged under
the doorway. With an **angry hiss**, this vile vegetation
wiggled sideways, grabbing at empty air, then it
retreated into the gardens.

'**HA!** We did it! We escaped!' I spun Berty round, then
held my hand out to Broccoli to high-five. 'Go, Team Tiny!'

He blinked at me, his arms glued firmly to his sides.

That's when I remembered that we were no longer
an **inventor-apprentice team**. 'Oh – uh –' I dropped my
hand as if I'd been stung. 'Well – uh – that was –
I'm **never** going to look at a plant in the
same way ever again,' I joked awkwardly.

Broccoli sniffed.

'Uh – well – thank you for – uh – coming back,' I said.
'I had the situation **under control**, but—'

'You did?' said Broccoli, raising an eyebrow.

'Oh, yes,' I said. 'Totally. But – uh – thank you
anyway.'

He shrugged. 'Well, I couldn't let a plant eat you, could I? It wouldn't have been the responsible thing to do and the T.W.S. says that tortoise owners must always be responsible. Besides, imagine what your mum and dad would have said.' He sniffed. 'Imagine what *my* mum and dad would have said.'

I nodded. For a teensy-tiny moment, I'd almost-sort of ~~hoped~~ thought that Broccoli had come back because he'd been worried about *me*. 'Well, there's Lift X.' I pointed to a shiny blue door in the middle of the corridor. 'We made it.'

'**Fifteen minutes** left to big ourselves,' said Broccoli. He frowned. 'We need to work out how to reach that call button, Archie.'

'That's exactly what I was think—' I began, then stopped. Not being an inventor-apprentice team still felt *extremely peculiar*. I cleared my throat and glanced around the corridor. A short distance ahead of us was a door marked **STOREROOM**.

BINGO.

'Look, Archie,' said Broccoli, pointing to the storeroom. 'There has to be something in there we can use to reach that call—'

Before he could finish speaking, the door to the
STOREROOM swung open.

'We need to get this stuff to the fifth floor,'
shouted a spacesuit, wheeling a trolley
into the corridor. 'The professor wants
it in the Weather Simulation Room *now* and he
doesn't like waiting.'

'Hang on,' shouted another voice. 'I've got a
few more coils to load up.'

I stared at the spacesuit, 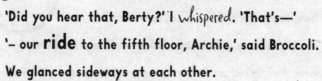 a brand-new
glittering idea

 lighting up my brain cells.

'Did you hear that, Berty?' I whispered. 'That's—'

'– our **ride** to the fifth floor, Archie,' said Broccoli.

We glanced sideways at each other.

Archibald looked between the two of us and did the
BIGGEST eye roll I'd ever seen.

Berty nudged my arm and whined.

I looked at the spacesuit a moment longer, then I turned
round to Broccoli. 'Ernie's got the molecular modulator.'

Broccoli's eyes **widened**. 'What? How do you know?'

I pulled out the tracker (which was still, annoyingly, not

working) and waved it at him. 'I heard it on this. He's going to come after the RoarEasy again.' I took a deep breath. 'I know you're not my apprentice any more, but I think – I think that maybe – we should *work together*.'

Broccoli sniffed. 'Together?'

'Only until we've **bigged** ourselves and changed Monsieur Crépeau back,' I added quickly. 'I'm not asking you to be my apprentice again.'

'No,' said Broccoli with another sniff.

'Absolutely not.'

'Because you wouldn't.'

I shook my head *furiously*. 'No.'

'And I wouldn't want to be.'

'Exactly. But we both want to be bigged or we'll stay shrunk forever. And neither of us wants the world to find out about what we did to Monsieur Crépeau.'

'No,' said Broccoli.

'*Practically*, it makes sense for us to stick together for now. We big ourselves, get the molecular modulator off Ernie and change Monsieur Crépeau back. After that, we never have to work with each other again.' I held out my hand to him. '**Deal?**'

Broccoli thought for a moment, then he sniffed and shook my hand. **'Deal.'**

'Hurry up, will you! The professor's waiting!' said the first spacesuit.

'Here you go,' said the second, loading a pile of **enormous** METAL COILS on to the trolley. 'That's the last of them.'

'That's our signal, Broccoli!' I said. I lifted Berty into the Transporter and swung it over my shoulder. Clutching the rucksack, I sprinted across the floor towards the spacesuit.

(Another BRILLIANT thing about being teensy-tiny: it's a lot easier to get around without being seen.)

'Come on! Or we'll miss our ride!'

The Big-o-Meter AKA
the Fifth Floor (FINALLY)

Broccoli has pointed out that you, the Reader, must be foot-hoppingly desperate to know exactly how we reached the fifth floor. Unfortunately, Berty got hold of these chronicles and **gobbled** through my very long and extremely **genius** explanation. Even more unfortunately, I don't have time to explain again (**genius inventors** are **busy**, after all), so I've included a quick summary instead:

① We almost got squished by one pair of human shoes.

② Make that two pairs.

③ We hitched a ride on a trolley.

[A note from Broccoli: If you, the Reader, should ever find yourself shrunk, I would not advise you to hitch a lift on a moving trolley. It is extremely dangerous and highly likely you could fall off and get squashed.]

Lift X drew to a halt with a loud **DING**.

'Get ready, Broccoli,' I whispered. As we entered the corridor, I leapt off the trolley on to the floor. There was a loud shriek, then a **thump** as Broccoli landed beside me.

'The fifth floor,' I said, pulling him to his feet. 'We're finally here.'

'BEEEUAHHHAE,' mumbled Broccoli. He looked positively AIRSICK. 'I'm not doing that again.'

I shook the pet tracker, but it was still blank. EUGH.

'The Big-o-Meter should be at the end of this corridor,' I said, checking the map.

'Uh – Esha?' said Broccoli.

My mouth dropped as I turned round. The corridor was in CHAOS. Weather spacesuits ran in and out of an **enormous** circular door, carrying buckets of snowflakes and cloudy wisps.

'Get this cleaned up!' shouted a voice from inside the room. 'The TV crew will be here to see the Weather Simulation Room in twenty minutes!'

'Twenty minutes?' echoed Broccoli. 'We still have to find Monsieur Crépeau and the molecular modulator before then.'

'Actually, I don't think we need to worry about that any more,' I said. 'Look.' Hovering in the air, not far above our heads, was the unmistakeable shape of a buzz-bot. *A buzz-bot that was looking directly at* **US**. 'Ernie's already found us.'

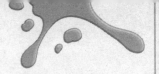

Broccoli's snot dropped a centimetre, his face paling.

I grabbed hold of his sleeve and pulled him forward.
'Come on! We've only got **TEN MINUTES** left to **big** ourselves.
If Ernie gets here before then, we don't stand a chance.'

Spacesuits lumbered above us like giant planets as
we scurried along the edge of the corridor. Shoes **THUD-
THUDDED** across the floor, each movement shaking my teensy-
tiny bones. Berty whined, the tip of his tail flicking worriedly.

'What do you mean there's a problem with the wind
generator?' **thundered** a voice as we passed the
Weather Simulation Room. A sequence of peculiar **RUMBLES**
and **BANGS** streamed through the doorway.

Peering inside, I caught a glimpse of a $TALL$ man.
He was built like a rubber band, with neatly trimmed
hair, thick glasses and a bushy beard, which was tied into
ringlets. 'The TV crew will be here shortly, and I, Professor
Rathbone, have promised to show them the scientific
breakthrough of the century. And — be careful with that!
Do you want to start a **WEATHERNOVA**? Do you have any
idea what it could DO?

DESTROY the WHOLE WORLD, THAT'S WHAT!'

Archibald snickered in excitement.

'And get this floor cleared! I want it empty for when the cameras arrive.'

More weather spacesuits hurried past us.

'TV crew will be arriving in twenty minutes for the Weather Simulation Room demo,' they announced, knocking on the doors around us. 'Please clear the floor.'

'There it is!' I whispered, my inventor's instincts tingling with excitement as I spotted a door marked BIG-O-METER.

'Oh no,' breathed Broccoli as a flood of spacesuits suddenly emerged from the other rooms and headed towards Lift X. Pressing myself flat against the wall, I scuttled sideways, the spacesuits marching so close that I could feel the swish of their clothes against my face. The buzz-bot darted between them, tracking our every move.

We were only a few tiny steps away from the Big-o-Meter room when the door suddenly flung open. Broccoli yanked me out of the way as an **enormous** boot came down on to the floor.

'WHY CAN'T YOU WATCH WHERE YOU'RE GOING?' I yelled, glancing up at a spacesuit.

'– don't know what the problem is,' he was

saying, clearly oblivious to the fact that he had almost CRUSHED a genius. 'We'll have to check it again after the TV crew have been –'

I didn't wait to hear any more.

Grabbing hold of Broccoli, I darted round the spacesuit's shoes and threw myself inside the room. The door swung closed, shutting off the noise in the corridor.

'There it is, Broccoli,' I whispered. **'The Big-o-Meter.'**

☆ It was **BEAUTIFUL.** ✹ ☆

It looked like a giant Hoover with a yellow whisk-shaped device fitted to the top. On the front was a button marked BIG. Next to it were several dials with numbers written next to them.

'No buzz-bot,' said Broccoli, glancing up. 'We must've left it outside.'

'Doesn't matter,' I said. 'Ernie already knows where we are.' Hurrying towards the Big-o-Meter, I reached up to the button marked BIG – at least, I *tried* to reach it.

'It's too high!' I grunted as I leapt up towards it.

Broccoli hesitated, then he held out his palms to give me a leg-up.

'Thank you,' I said awkwardly.

Teetering a little, I climbed up on to his hand and pushed the button.

Nothing
happened.

Archibald snickered gleefully.

'It's not working,' I said, a *horrible panic* creeping over me.

'Press it again,' panted Broccoli.

Still nothing.

Berty whined.

I tried again for a third time, my heart sinking to the bottom of my shoes. Being compacted might have been one of the **COOLEST** things to ever happen to me, but I didn't want to stay shrunk FOREVER. That thought was nearly worse than being disqualified from the Young Inventor of the Year contest.

'Esha, wait,' said Broccoli. At the side of the machine was an arrow pointing to the bottom of the Big-o-Meter. Next to the arrow was the word: **POWER.** As we peered under the machine, my eye fell on a yellow switch that was flicked to **OFF.**

That's when the door behind us opened.

I whirled round, my inventor's instincts twitching with impatience as Ernie stepped into the room. 2.0 came in after him. **CLANK CLUNK.** In Ernie's hand was a basket with an irritated Monsieur Crépeau inside it.

'Found you,' said Ernie, with an ULTRA-ANNOYING smirk on his face.

Broccoli stepped back, his hand sliding under the Big-o-Meter.

'Took you long enough,' I retorted, stepping in front of him.

Ernie scowled. 'I should have known you'd be coming here. You owe me a spi-droid.'

'And you owe me a Slimer Shot.'

'My uncle told me everything I needed to know.' He waved a shiny purple object at us. 'I have the molecular modulator. Give me your translation device and I'll make sure 2.0 doesn't squa—'

Suddenly the Big-o-Meter hummed to life behind me.

Ernie's eyes narrowed. 'Grab them, 2.0.'

Berty **roared,** terrified, as 2.0 clanked forward.

'Hurry up, Esha!' shouted Broccoli, holding out his hands to give me a leg-up. We've only got a few minutes left!' I leapt on to his palms and punched my fist against the BIG button.

With a loud **GLUG–GLUG**, the Big-o-Meter sprang into action: the whisk-like device spun wildly, a small panel slid back on the front of the machine and a circle of light, marked TARGET AREA, shone on to the floor.

'BIG-O-METER ACTIVE,' said an automated voice. 'PLEASE SELECT YOUR SETTING.'

CLANK CLUNK.

There was a worried warble from the basket.

Before I could choose a setting, the Big-o-Meter hissed loudly.

2.0's hand reached down towards me, then –

BOOM!

An **enormous** pulse of energy rocketed out of the device.

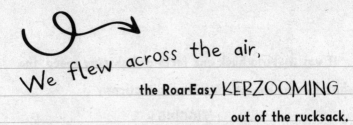

We flew across the air, the RoarEasy KERZOOMING out of the rucksack.

The pet tracker whizzed out of my pocket.

Ernie and 2.0 hit a wall with a loud **THUD –**

CLUNK!

Monsieur Crépeau whizzed out of Ernie's basket and slid across the floor. Berty flew out of the Transporter with a frightened roar.

'Ow,' groaned Broccoli as we landed with a **THUMP** on the carpet. Archibald poked his head out of his shell and grinned wickedly. 'What was *that?*'

'No idea.' I leapt to my feet and scanned the room. 'There's the RoarEasy,' I said, pointing to a teensy-tiny object in the centre of the carpet.

The Big-o-Meter **did not** look good.

In fact, it looked like a volcano that was about to

ERUPT.

It was shaking back and forth at lightning speed, the whisk-like device rotating in all directions.

'BIGGING –

BIGGING –

STAND CLEAR.'

The BIG button popped off the front and shot across the room, narrowly missing the top of Monsieur Crépeau's head. He blinked at me in outrage.

'Checking systems for damage,' rasped 2.0.

Ernie groaned as he sat up.

A deep **WHUMP** echoed from inside the Big-o-Meter. The orange circle of light flickered once, twice, then turned off completely. Without warning, the whisk-like device juddered to a standstill, pointing directly at us. The dials spun wildly.

'System check complete,' said 2.0. 'No damage detected.'

'BIGGING –

BIGGING –

SETTING FIVE.'

Before either of us could move,
a bolt of green shot out
and ZAPPED Broccoli.

'Esha!' he screamed as he flew into the air.

'W-h-a-t's h-a-p-p-en-ing?'

I watched, open-mouthed, as Broccoli GREW in front
of my eyeballs. First his legs extended, then his arms
elongated, then his neck and head shot up towards the
ceiling, his whole body

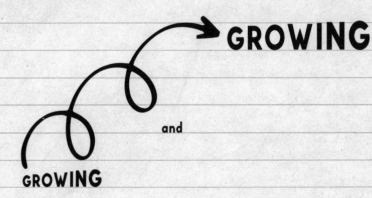

GROWING

and

GROWING

until I was looking
at this . . .

Shocked
Esha

I breathed in sharply. My ex-apprentice and his evil pet were GIGANTIC. They loomed far above my head, taking up almost half the room. Berty squealed in surprise. Archibald's eyes widened as he glanced at his superior size, then he grinned down at me with an EVIL smirk and made a noise that sounded like, 'this is more like it'. I shuddered. Forget dinosaurs. A GINORMOUS TORTOISE was the stuff of reptilian NIGHTMARES.

'Esha?' whimpered Broccoli. A blob of snot, the size of an enormous hailstone, dropped on to the floor with a sticky SPLASH.

'What's happening?' gasped Ernie.

'Excess energy detected,' said 2.0. 'Conclusion: device malfunction.'

'I can see that, 2.0!' snapped Ernie impatiently. A cloud of orange smoke was streaming out of the Big-o-Meter. It huff-puffed out of the top, filling the entire room.

'Esha, do something!' squealed Broccoli. 'It's too high up here.' He sneezed, showering us with a sticky fountain of snot.

'Hold on,' I shouted, sprinting towards the Big-o-Meter. Berty bounded beside me, his tail flicking in excitement.

'We have to figure out how to resize Broccoli and ourselves, Berty!' I said.

Broccoli sneezed again, sending a storm of snot spraying over us.

SPLAT!

Some landed on Monsieur Crépeau, who was glaring at us as if he wanted to vaporize us on the spot.

Some almost landed on Ernie, who dived out of its way just in time.

'BIGGING – BIGGING – SETTING TWO.'
PERWHIZZZ!

A bolt of green whizzed towards me. A moment later, I was thrown into the air. Out of the corner of my eye, I caught a glimpse of Berty flying up alongside me, his amber eyes wide with fright.

I felt warm, cold, warm again, then a peculiar sensation took hold of me. Every part of my body felt as if it were being s-t-r-e-t-c-h-e-d o-u-t-w-a-r-d-s, first my fingers, then my arms, then toes, legs, head, everything tickling and tingling as it extended further and further until, with a loud POP, it stopped.

'OOF!' I groaned as I fell to the floor.

I looked down at my hands and feet in spingly-tingly realization.

I'd been (BIGGED.) Not BIGGED like Broccoli into a giant. I'd been BIGGED to my normal height (give or take a few centimetres).

'I'm back,' I breathed, unable to believe my eyes. Berty was still floating in the air above my head. He roared in panic, snapping at the sparks with his teeth. Without warning, the Big-o-Meter suddenly let off a small **bang,** dropping Berty on to the floor. He inspected his puppy dimensions and **roared** in delight.

'BIGGING – BIGGING – **SETTING TWO.'**

Another bolt of green fired out and hit the RoarEasy, which grew, bigger and **bigger,** until it was back to its normal size.

'Come on, Berty!' I shouted, darting towards it.

There was a loud **whirr.** Glancing left, I saw 2.0 moving in my direction, his green eyes flickering as they locked on to me. I sprinted through the smoke towards the RoarEasy. Berty galloped along beside me with a delighted **ROAR.**

(I'm not entirely sure he understood the urgency of our situation.)

CLUNK CLUNK.

My stomach flip-twisted as I saw 2.0 marching towards me.

'Broccoli, get the molecular modulator!' I shouted.

'I can't see Ernie!' he squealed. 'There's too much smoke!'

With **genius** acrobatics, I dodged another bolt of green and dived towards the RoarEasy.

Too late.

Before I could grab hold of it, Ernie dived through the smoke and snatched up my **genius invention**, Monsieur Crépeau held under his arm.

'SQUAWK!' warbled Monsieur Crépeau as Ernie **ran** towards the door.

'Wait till the world sees me change Monsieur Crépeau back into a human!' shouted Ernie, disappearing out of the room. 'You'll never be able to call yourself an inventor again!'

That's when the Big-o-Meter went completely and

utterly **MAD.**

It leapt into the air, bolts of green flying about in all directions in the most spectacular LASER LIGHT show. One hit 2.0, who began to shake on the spot.

'System alert,' rasped the robot. His ears spun and his eyes flashed. 'System alert.'

'BIGGING – BIGGING – SETTING TWO.'

Another bolt zapped Broccoli and Archibald, who suddenly dropped down into the smoke, out of sight.

'ESHAAAAAA!' shrieked Broccoli.

I looked at the door, every one of my inventor's instincts itching to go after Ernie immediately, then I pulled myself away and sprinted back through the smoke for my ex-apprentice.

'ESHA! YOU WON'T BELIEVE IT!'

Quite certain that something terrible had happened to Broccoli, I raced towards the sound of his voice and saw . . .

that he had completely and utterly disappeared.

[A note from Broccoli: Ahem.]

OK, OK, I'm joking. That's what I thought might have happened. What had *actually* happened was that Broccoli (and his evil tortoise) had returned to their normal size.

'We're back!' said Broccoli. He sneezed with happiness and hugged Archibald close to his chest. 'Can you believe it, Archie? We're REALLY back!'

Archibald looked at his small claws and rolled his eyes in disgust.

'SYSTEM ALERT,' rasped 2.0. 'ALERT – ALERT – AL—'

I *GOGGLED* as 2.0 started to **GROW**.

First his metal legs –

next, his metal arms –

then his metal head –

I grabbed hold of Broccoli and pulled him towards the door. 'We have to get to the Weather Simulation Room

 # The Weather Simulation Room

We sprinted out just in time to see Ernie dive into the Weather Simulation Room. Our footsteps **THUDDED** across the now-empty corridor as we sped after him.

'Where's everyone gone?' panted Broccoli behind me.

'They cleared the floor, remember!'

A speaker crackled above us.

 'The *SCIENCE TODAY* TV crew will be here in eight minutes. All laboratory staff are reminded to make their way to the entrance for their arrival.'

CLANK CLUNK.

The floor shuddered beneath us.

Broccoli gasped. **'ESHA!'**

Glancing over my shoulder, I saw 2.0 wobble into the corridor after us.

My mouth d
      r
       o
        p
        ped.

He was

ENORMOUS.

He towered into the air at almost **DOUBLE** his normal

height, his arms and legs swaying unsteadily as he

lumbered after us.

CLANK CLUNK.

Paint and plaster fell across the floor as his springy

hair scraped the ceiling. His eyes flashed like huge

headlights, his ears *whirring* like helicopters.

EUGH.

(As if a normal-sized robot wasn't **BAD ENOUGH**.)

With a burst of lightning speed, I charged towards the

Weather Simulation Room, yanked open the door and . . .

came face to face with an ICE MONSTER.

[A note from Broccoli: ESHA!]

Oh, wait, that's a different journal . . .

This, dear Reader, is what I saw on the other side . . .

In front of us were at least ten cylinders, each one TALL and transparent with a MIND-BOGGLING concoction of colours swirling inside it. Each cylinder rattled and hissed softly as if the concoction inside were trying to break out. At the bottom of each cylinder was a shiny brass weather dial.

A burst of turquoise grey suddenly flashed past me from the other side of the room.

'Monsieur Crépeau?' squeaked Broccoli as our pigeoned teacher darted across the floor, his feet slapping against the ground with impressive speed.

'GET BACK HERE!' shouted Ernie, darting after him. His T-shirt was splattered with pigeon poop. The RoarEasy was wedged inside his belt. 'I'M GOING TO CHANGE YOU BACK IN FRONT OF THE WHOLE WORLD!'

Monsieur Crépeau squawked loudly as if to say, 'I don't think so'. His wings flapped furiously, faster and faster, until, as if by a spark of bewildering BEAUTIFUL MAGIC,

he FLEW into the air,

the molecular modulator gleaming purple in his beak.

A **SPINGLY-TINGLY** shiver ran down my spine.

'NO WAY,' I gasped in delight.

(Cracking the secret of flight was probably
the **COOLEST** thing Monsieur Crépeau had *ever* done.)

'He finally figured it out,' breathed Broccoli behind me.

Before either of us could move, Ernie whipped out a
robotic contraption from his inventor's belt.

SKIIIINNGGGGGGG!

It squealed through the air with surprising speed. As
it reached Monsieur Crépeau, a hook shot out at one end.
The tip nudged Monsieur Crépeau's foot. With a **HEART-
DROPPING** squawk, he tumbled through the air and
landed on the ground in a dizzy heap. The molecular
modulator whizzed out of his beak, flew across the room
and landed perfectly on top of a weather cylinder.

Ernie glanced at the molecular modulator, then back
at me. With an **EVIL** glint in his eyes, he sprinted
towards it.

Archibald made a noise that sounded like, **'fight!'**.

'I'LL GET MONSIEUR CRÉPEAU!' shouted Broccoli.

'AND I'LL DEAL WITH ERNIE!' I said, darting after him.

Ernie leapt on to the control panel, his robotic contraption aimed at the molecular modulator. I jumped on after him and grabbed hold of the metal rod.

'GET OFF, VERMA!' he snarled, clutching tightly to the other end. 'THIS IS *MY* PINCER PINCH!'

Berty glanced from Ernie to me, and back again, whining softly.

CLANK. CLUNK!

The cylinders shook as 2.0 drew closer.

'I SAID GET OFF!' shouted Ernie. With annoying strength, he yanked the Pincer Pinch out of my hands. My arms flapped in a **wild wobble** as I tried to keep my balance. My foot slid across the dial.

'SNOW FUNCTION ENGAGED,' said an automated voice. The cylinder rattled faster, the whole thing shaking like a bottle of pop about to EXPLODE. Berty squealed as a stream of snow began pumping out of the top.

KERZIIIING!

Ernie's Pincer Pinch shot past my face towards the top of the cylinder.

'Oh no you don't,' I hissed. With **ROCKET** speed, I threw myself at him, knocking him off the control panel.

'NO!' shouted Ernie as the Pincer Pinch hit the cylinder, wedging itself in the glass with a

horrible CRACK —

'ESHA, I'VE GOT MONSIEUR CRÉPEAU!' shouted Broccoli.

A fountain of snow spurted upwards into the air, throwing the molecular modulator across the room. Broccoli leapt after it, Monsieur Crépeau held under his arm. With **genius-level** quick thinking, I snatched the RoarEasy from Ernie's belt and jumped to my feet.

'Can you see it, Broccoli?' I shouted, squinting through the snow.

'Not yet!' he shrieked. His orange hair bounced wildly as he searched. With an irritated squawk, Monsieur Crépeau wriggled out from under his arm, landed beside him and began poking the snow with his beak.

'NO,

NO,

NO!' shrieked Ernie,

desperately trying to pull the Pincer Pinch out of the cylinder. 'Uncle Rathbone's going to be *furious!*'

CLANK CLUNK.

My heart d*ropped* between my toes as 2.0's shadow fell across the doorway. A moment later, an enormous robot foot stepped inside the room. This was followed by a ginormous robot leg, then the rest of 2.0, his metal frame towering over us in a splendid spectacle of steel.

[A note from Broccoli: Splendid isn't the word I would use to describe it. Terrifying, maybe.]

'2.0!' gasped Ernie. 'YOU BIGGED YOURSELF? HOW –'
Suddenly a VILLAINOUS SMIRK twisted across his face.
'YOU BIGGED YOURSELF!' He pointed in our direction.

'GET THEM, 2.0!'

'FOUND IT!' shouted Broccoli, waving the molecular modulator at me. Two snowy caterpillars had formed on his eyebrows.

I leapt out of the way as 2.0's hand came down towards me. With a fierce **ROAR**, Berty charged towards the robot. I watched in amazement as my usually scaredy dino clamped his jaws on his metal fingers.

'CAREFUL, 2.0!' shouted Ernie as the robot reared backwards, Berty clinging on to his hand.

'SYSTEM ALERT,' said the robot. 'SYSTEM ALERT.'

'FINALLY!' snarled Ernie, pulling the Pincer Pinch free. A stream of snow pumped out of the crack. He hopped off the control panel and strode towards me. 'A **genius inventor** has to do everything themselves. Give me the translation device, Esha.'

A single, ZINGING SPARK suddenly lit up my brain cells.

'No, they don't,' I murmured. Spinning on the spot, I threw the RoarEasy towards my ex-apprentice. 'CATCH IT, BROCCOLI!' I shouted.

The RoarEasy whizzed through the air and . . .

dropped into the snow.

'I TOLD YOU TO CATCH IT!'

'YOU DIDN'T GIVE ME ENOUGH WARNING!' yelled Broccoli.

2.0 wavered unsteadily as Berty scampered up his arm towards his neck.

More *cracks* **EXPLODED** through the air as the snow forced itself through the cylinder. Ernie's face twisted into a **scowl.** His Pincer Pinch clacked with **menace** as he came towards me. 'This is all your fault, Verm-AAAAAAAAAA!'

A **thunderous jet of snow** suddenly spurted from the side of the cylinder, knocking him sideways.

'I'VE GOT THE ROAREASY, ESHA!' shouted Broccoli.

I ducked as a second fountain of snow shot out, then a third and a fourth, until a stream of snow jets were ZINGING out of the cylinder like rockets.

'FIX THE MOLECULAR MODULATOR TO IT!'

'I DON'T KNOW HOW – YOU HAVE TO TELL ME WHAT TO DO!'

'YOU RESTARTED A SPI-DROID!' I yelled, crawling towards the control panel. The snow whirled around my face, stinging my eyes and cheeks. If I didn't stop it soon, we'd all be swallowed inside an AVALANCHE.

'YOU FIGURED OUT HOW TO ESCAPE THE JAR AND YOU ARE THE BEST TORTOISE OWNER IN THE COUNTRY. YOU CAN WORK IT OUT!'

Before I could reach the control panel, a dial popped off and shot across the room.

'WARNING – SNOW VALVE FAILURE – WARNING.'

'I DON'T KNOW IF I CAN!' squeaked Broccoli.

'BUT I DO!' I bellowed.

'I TRUST YOU, BROCCOLI!'

'YOU DO?'

'EURGH!' spluttered Ernie furiously as he shot up from under a mini mountain of snow, shaking it off around him.

I ducked out of the way as 2.0's hand scraped against the control panel.

'WARNING – WIND FUNCTION ENGAGED – WARNING –'

A sudden, powerful gust of wind roared between my arms and legs.

'HURRY UP!' I shouted.

'I'M TRYING!' he *squeaked*.

Clank-clanking, 2.0 swung round on the spot, his arm *whirring* upwards as Berty darted on to his shoulder. I leapt to the right, Ernie diving to the left as 2.0's foot slammed to the floor. The Pincer Pinch fell down between us into the snow.

'SQUAWK!'

Monsieur Crépeau's eyes **widened** as 2.0's foot swung round on top of him and

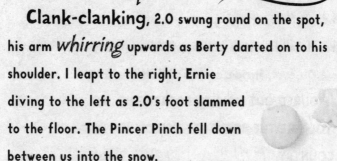

SQUASHED HIM

to

PIGEON PULP.

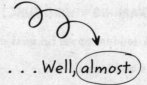

. . . Well, almost.

With remarkable timing (and bravery), I leapt forward and snatched hold of Ernie's Pincer Pinch.

BA-ZING!

It whizzed forward and BOPPED Monsieur Crépeau away from 2.0's foot. He slid across the floor with a dizzy squawk.

'I THINK I'M ALMOST – THERE!' Broccoli grinned as he waved the RoarEasy at me. His snot had almost frozen into an icicle. 'I THINK I'VE DONE IT!' ←

'GIVE ME THAT!' yelled Ernie, stomping towards Broccoli like a wild snowman.

KERZIIIING!

I aimed the Pincer Pinch at his feet and sent him tumbling back down again.

'NOW, BROCCOLI!' I shouted.

'NO!' cried Ernie as a bolt of purple whizzomed out of the RoarEasy and hit Monsieur Crépeau, who fell backwards, his wings circling wildly in the air.

'YES!' I yelled. **'WE'VE DONE IT! WE'VE DONE – OH,'** I finished as I stared at the still-pigeoned Monsieur Crépeau. He blinked at his wings, then back at me, his moustache drooping sadly.

Broccoli's face dropped in disappointment. 'It didn't work!'

'TRY IT AGAIN!' I shouted.

That's when 2.0 SLIPPED.

His foot slithered across the snow, his entire body

creaking as he F
E
L
L.

'MOVE, BROCCOLI!' I shouted, diving out of the way.

He scooped up Monsieur Crépeau and Archibald and

leapt sideways, narrowly missing being SQUISHED by 2.0's

enormous body as it came down towards us.

The robot's hand slid across the control panel with a loud

CLUNK-CLUNK.

Berty appeared on 2.0's shoulder and charged down his arm.

'WARNING – MULTIPLE WEATHER FUNCTIONS SELECTED –

EVASIVE ACTION RECOMMENDED – WARNING –'

UH-OH.

With a

SPECTACULAR LEAP,

Berty flew through the air towards me.

'Gotcha!' I shouted, catching him in my arms.

'SYSTEM UNSTEADY – SYSTEM UNSTEADY –' garbled 2.0 as he landed with a **ginormous THUD.**

The entire Weather Simulation Room shook, the cylinders rattling with the force of his weight.

'SYSTEM DAMAGE DETECTED – SYSTEM DAMAGE DETECTED –' rasped 2.0.

'2.0!' shouted Ernie, darting towards him.

Broccoli wobbled up from behind 2.0's leg, a smirking Archibald and a dizzy Monsieur Crépeau clutched in his arms.

'What is *that*?' he gasped, pointing upwards.

I followed his hand.

My heart dropped down to my toes.

'WARNING – WEATHERNOVA DETECTED –

WARNING –

WEATHERNOVA–'

The Weathernova

There, right before my eyes, a *tornado* had started to form above us.

The air spun into a **STORMY BLACK VORTEX,**

pulling on the weather streaming out of the cylinders.

Bright bolts of **lightning**

CRACKLED

between showers of sleet.

Snow whirled around hail bursts.

Rain spun into sunshine.

Thunder echoed between

clouds of fog,

the wind whipping everything together

into a

CRASHING,

COILING

CONCOCTION.

My ears P^OPPED as I stood up.

'WARNING – WEATHERNOVA DETECTED –

WARNING – WEATHERNOVA—'

Berty whined and ducked behind 2.0's arm, which was

bent across the floor in front of us.

'Oh no,' breathed Ernie behind me.

For the first time ever, my **arch-nemesis**

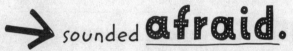 sounded **afraid.**

'My uncle warned me about this.'

 The wind whooshed around us in a

HAIR-RAISING HOWL.

The RoarEasy whizzed out of Broccoli's hands

and disappeared into the

V
O
R
T
E
X.

'**NO!**' he shrieked, lurching forward. '**NOT THE ROAREASY!**'

'**STAY BACK, BROCCOLI!**' I yelled.

'**BUT WE CAN'T CHANGE MONSIEUR CRÉPEAU BACK WITHOUT—**'

With a heart-stopping CRACK, a cylinder tore away from the control panel and whizzed into the centre of the vortex, collapsing into teensy-tiny pieces. The weathernova pulsed a fierce purple colour, the whole thing expanding with a BEASTLY **roar.**

Monsieur Crépeau squawked in terror.

'**WE HAVE BIGGER THINGS TO WORRY ABOUT RIGHT NOW!**' I yelled.

(After all, Monsieur Crépeau being a pigeon was definitely less trouble than being *disintegrated* by a weathernova.)

Archibald drummed his claws in glee.

'I have to **stop it,**' shrieked Ernie. 'Uncle Rathbone will never forgive me if it gets out. It could swallow *everything.*'

That's when he did something unbelievably RIDICULOUS.

He charged through the snow *towards* the weathernova.

'ERNIE, WHAT ARE YOU DOING?' I yelled.

'THERE'S A

MASTER SWITCH

UNDER THE CONTROL PANEL FOR EMER—'

Another cylinder **ripped off** the control panel and whirled into the weathernova.

It **THUNDERED** loudly and pulsed a violent green. The wind twisted even faster, whipping Ernie off his feet.

'**AAAAARRGGHHH!**' he screamed as he flew towards the centre of the vortex.

Talk about being a TOTAL air-brain.

'ERNIE!' shrieked Broccoli.

I clambered over 2.0's arm and aimed the Pincer Pinch towards my arch-nemesis.

(OK, I am sure that you, the Reader, are wondering why I bothered to save Rat-Bone. But I could hardly let him get sucked into a weathernova, could I? Not when I could rescue him and BOAST about it after.)

KERZIING!

It shot out towards him, the hook clamping around his leg.

'OW!' he bellowed.

The Pincer Pinch creaked in my hand as the weathernova tugged me forward. I jabbed the button to pull him back, but the Pincer Pinch was caught in the windstorm now. It groaned against the force of the weathernova, the whole thing rattling in my hands.

'IT'S – TOO – STRONG,' I grunted as the wind pulled me forward. 'I CAN'T HOLD—'

Suddenly I felt a pair of hands grab on to me.

'GOT YOU!' shouted Broccoli.

Archibald made a noise that sounded like, 'you'll never make it, humans'.

'PULL!' I shouted.

'HURRY UP, WORMS!' screeched Ernie.

'WHAT DO YOU THINK WE'RE DOING?' I bellowed.

The wind roared around us, stinging my cheeks and hands.

'PULL, BROCCOLI!'

'I'm trying!' he shrieked, his feet scrabbling across the snow. Monsieur Crépeau flapped his wings, (unhelpfully) squawking commands.

We slid forward, battling helplessly against the force of the wind, the weathernova fizzing and crackling. Suddenly I felt something **tug** us backwards.

'THAT'S IT, BERTY!' shouted Broccoli. 'GOOD BOY! PULL, BERTY! GO ON!'

Glancing over my shoulder, I saw Berty's teeth clamped on Broccoli's trouser leg, his tail curled round 2.0's arm. Step by slow step, we dragged Ernie **away** from the vortex, the Pincer Pinch **groaning** under his weight.

'ALMOST THERE!' I grunted.

With a final, **painful groan,** the Pincer Pinch snapped in **HALF.** I leapt forward to grab Ernie's hand, the other end of the Pincer Pinch whirling away into the vortex as we dragged ourselves behind 2.0. We crouched down beside the robot's enormous arm, his metal frame sheltering us from the wind storm.

'You **broke** my Pincer Pinch,' panted Ernie.

'We also SAVED you,' I pointed out.

'SYSTEMS FAILING,' rasped 2.0. His eyes flashed, his ears spinning weakly before coming to a halt. 'SYSTEMS FAILING. SYSTEMS FAILING –'

'2.0!' shouted Ernie. He turned on me, his lip wobbling. **'This is your fault, Verma!'**

'Is now really the time to be pointing **FINGERS?**' I yelled as a powerful gust of wind *ripped* out the remaining weather cylinders and part of the control panel.

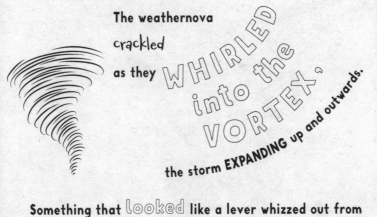

The weathernova crackled as they WHIRLED into the VORTEX, the storm EXPANDING up and outwards.

Something that looked like a lever whizzed out from the wall and disappeared into the roaring winds.

'The MASTER SWITCH!' wailed Ernie. His face paled. 'We're *never* going to be able to **stop it** now.'

'There **must** be some way to contain it!' said Broccoli.

'Like what?' shrieked Ernie.

I stuck my hand into my Inventor's Kit before remembering that everything had fallen out at the Botanical Gardens. All I had left was Berty's T-rex Transporter and his Pooper Scooper.

How UNHELPFUL.

'What have you got in your Inventor's Belt, Rat-Bone?' I said.

His hands shook as he pulled out a handful of wires, coils and a few Allen keys.

My heart sank. 'That's it?'

'I didn't know I was going to be dealing with a weathernova, did I?' he snapped.

'SYSTEMS FAILING – SYSTEMS FAILING,' rasped 2.0.

I swallowed. Being digested by a Guzzler was one thing. Releasing a weathernova that could

destroy the WHOLE world was quite another.

My brain *whirred* desperately as I looked at what
was in front of us:

1. A Pooper Scooper
2. Wires
3. Coils
4. Allen keys.

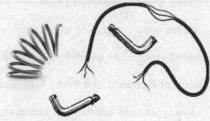

It was hardly enough to take on a WEATHERNOVA that
was growing **bigger** by the minute.

'There must be *something* we can do,' said Broccoli.

'What?' screeched Ernie. The weathernova rose
upwards, the ceiling rattling against its force. 'It's
sucking up everything!'

'SYSTEMS FAILING,' said 2.0. 'SYSTEMS FAILING.'

I stared at the robot, then at the Pooper Scooper,

a GOLDEN glittering idea
suddenly lighting up my brain cells.

'THAT'S IT!' I shouted. 'THAT'S WHAT
WE'LL DO. WE'LL **SUCK UP** THE SUCKER!'

'What are you talking about, Verma?' snapped Ernie.

I pulled Berty's Pooper Scooper out of the Transporter.
'**The Ultimate Suction Pooper Scooper,**' I
declared. 'Designed for the most dangerous and deathly

poop *imaginable*. We're going to hoover that weathernova.'

Broccoli stared at me. *'What?'*

'We're not going to contain it in that,' said Ernie incredulously. 'It's not **big** or **strong** enough.'

'We don't need to,' I said. 'We're going to use—'

'**2.0,**' said Broccoli, his face brightening in sudden understanding.

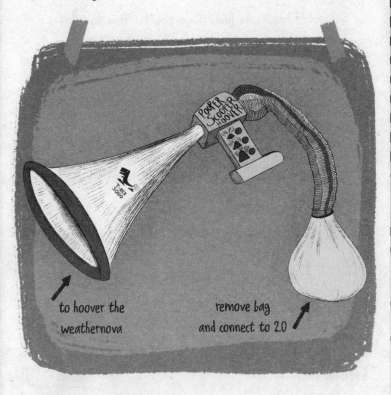

to hoover the
weathernova

remove bag
and connect to 2.0

Archibald HALOOTED, his whole body shaking with laughter.

Monsieur Crépeau squawked as if to say, 'that's the silliest idea I've ever heard'.

'Exactly.' I looked at Ernie. 'You said 2.0 has multiple connection ports, didn't you?' I waved the Pooper Scooper at him. 'Can you fix this to him?'

Ernie snorted. 'Course I can. I'm a **genius inventor**, Verma. But I'm not letting you use my robot for anything.'

'Don't be an AIR-BRAIN, Rat-Bone,' I retorted. 'We have to work together. The *Inventor's Handbook* says that the

BEST kind of inventing is done as a **TEAM**.'

'**No, it doesn't,**' said Ernie.

'Well, it *should*,' I said. 'We might be ARCH-ENEMIES, but right now we've got a bigger problem.' I pointed at the weathernova. It snapped and popped above us, streaks of purple and green dancing towards the ceiling like a party of *electric eels*. 'Do you want that getting out?'

Ernie scowled and said nothing.

'You might not be as **genius** an inventor as me, but you're still an inventor,' I said. 'A **real** one. With *real inventions.*'

'That's not what my uncle thinks,' said Ernie quietly.

'So prove him wrong. Help us stop the weathernova.'

'How do you know it'll work?'

'I don't,' I said. 'But that's what inventing's about. Taking chances.'

Ernie opened his mouth as if he was about to argue.

'Unless *you* have a better idea?' I snapped.

'Fine,' he said through gritted teeth. 'But nobody touches 2.0 except me.'

'Done.' I ripped off the bag that was connected to the Pooper Scooper and pushed the end towards him. 'Fix that end to 2.0.'

'I don't take orders from—'

'**NOW, RAT-BONE!**' I yelled, pointing the Hoover end towards the weathernova.

Muttering under his breath, Ernie used an Allen key to open a control panel neatly hidden under 2.0's arm. His fingers moved with impressive

speed as he whipped the coils and
wires between the end of the Pooper
Scooper and 2.0.

'**Done!**' He put his hand on 2.0's arm. 'I'm sorry
about this, 2.0, but we don't have a choice. We can't let
the weathernova get out of this laboratory.'

'SYSTEMS FAILING – SYSTEMS FAILING.' The robot's eyes
flashed weakly.

The weathernova twisted above us in a
STOMACH-DROPPING SURGE.

I hesitated, feeling a cold flicker of uncertainty. Ernie was
right. We had no way of knowing if this was going to work.

'Chapter 35 of the *Inventor's Handbook*,' said Broccoli,
watching me. His fingers gripped the other end of the
Pooper Scooper tightly.

'What?'

'Chapter 35: the most important ingredient for any
inventor is—'

'**– a spark of faith,**' I finished slowly,
strangely relieved that Broccoli was beside me.

I looked at the weathernova and swallowed. 'You're right. Let's do this.'

Berty whined softly.

I jabbed the <u>ULTIMATE SUCTION</u> button.

For one teensy-tiny moment, nothing happened.

'It's not working!' shouted Rat-Bone behind us. 'I knew this was a dumb—'

With a jaw-rattling **WHOOSH,** the Pooper Scooper **came to life.**

'HOLD ON, BROCCOLIIIIIII!' I bellowed as the weathernova began to shift and swirl. A handful of snowy strands tugged free of the **vortex** and whizzed into the Pooper Scooper.

'SYSTEMS FAILING,' echoed 2.0. 'SYSTEMS FAILING –'

The weathernova continued upwards with a **loud ROAR,** crackling and sparking in front of us.

'IT'S TOO BIG!' I cried.

'WE NEED MORE POWER!' yelled Broccoli.

'It's on **Ultimate Suction** already!' I gasped, my heart sinking.

At that moment, Reader, when I was *absolutely sure* we were all DOOMED, I heard behind us a faint THUNK.

'THIS SHOULD HELP!' shouted Ernie. 'COME ON, 2.0! LET'S SUCK UP THAT SUCKER!'

'DIVERTING REMAINING POWER,' said 2.0's voice.

With a fearsome **THRUM**, the Pooper Scooper leapt into

ROCKET mode.

It tugged and pulled the air in front of us, the entire contraption shaking so fast that I was absolutely sure my arms were going to pop out of their sockets.

'That's done it!' I bellowed as more strands began to pull apart from the weathernova.

Monsieur Crépeau squawked, eyes wide in bewilderment, as the weathernova began to shrink.

'DIVERTING REMAINING POWER –' rasped 2.0's voice weakly.

The weathernova snapped and crackled, the whole thing **falling a** **P a r t** in glowing strands as the Pooper Scooper pulled it inwards. 2.0 rattled wildly as the weathernova entered his metal body.

'THAT'S IT!' whooped Ernie.

'IT'S WORKING!'

'DIVERTING REMAINING POWER –'

With a **final, angry crackle,** the last of the weathernova roared into the Pooper Scooper, stinging our faces as it rushed past.

Archibald grunted in disappointment.

'It worked!' I dropped the Pooper Scooper and pulled a teary-eyed Broccoli into a hug. 'It really worked!'

Berty squealed and thumped his tail against the floor in delight.

Monsieur Crépeau squawked in disbelief.

'DIVERTING REMAINING –' With a sad **VHOOMP,** 2.0 powered down into silence.

'I'm sorry, 2.0,' whispered Ernie behind us. His lip wobbled as he stared at the robot, two scarlet patches forming on his cheeks.

I swallowed. Stepping forward, I put my arm awkwardly round Ernie and patted him on the shoulder. 'I – um – I'm sorry, Rat— Ernie,' I said. '2.0 was a – um – genius invention. You—'

A loud rattling suddenly echoed from inside 2.0. We stumbled back as he rose upwards, the Pooper Scooper dangling in the air.

'What's happening?' gasped Broccoli.

2.0's eyes flashed, his ears whirring at top speed. His body jangled and shook. A few of the springs on his head popped off and clanged against the wall.

'SYSTEM POWER RESETTING – SYSTEM POWER RESETTING –'

'Resetting?' squeaked Ernie. 'How?'

'The weathernova energy,' I murmured.

We dived out of the way as 2.0's hand shot off his body and rocketed against the ceiling with a loud BANG. His head spun uncontrollably and I was absolutely certain that he was going to EXPLODE when, quite suddenly, he landed back on the snow with a loud **CLANK-CLANK**. He **wobbled** on the spot for a few moments, then stopped. His eyes flashed, his ears *whirring* at their normal speed.

Ernie's mouth dropped.

'**2.0,**' he gasped.

'**SYSTEM POWER RESET**, Master Rathbone,' said 2.0.

Ernie leapt forward and hugged 2.0's leg. 'It's good to have you back, 2.0,' he grinned.

'**ERNIE RATHBONE!**'

I looked up.

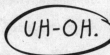

UH-OH.

What Happened Next

At the entrance to the Weather Simulation Room, in front of a bewildered audience, was Professor Rathbone. He looked **HOPPING MAD**.

'**WHAT HAPPENED HERE?**' he bellowed, striding through the snow. Cameras flashed and p^opped behind him. 'Well?' he demanded, stopping before us. 'What do you have to say for yourself, Ernie?'

'Well – I – um –' said Ernie.

DOOSH!

Broccoli suddenly p^opped out of the snow, his hands clutching Archibald. '*We made it!*' he gasped.

Archibald grunted in disappointment and disappeared into his shell.

DOOSH!

Berty burst out of the snow alongside him and licked Broccoli's face in delight.

The professor stared at them in silence.

The snow jiggled again.

DOOSH!

Monsieur Crépeau's HUMAN head popped out of the snow.

I GOGGLED.

Had it . . . ?

Could it be . . . ?

'It worked,' whispered Broccoli, who was staring at Monsieur Crépeau with his mouth open. Archibald poked a beady eyeball out of his shell and made a noise that sounded like, 'life is **SO** unfair'.

I grinned at my ~~apprentice~~ ex-apprentice. 'Knew you'd figure it out. Must've been a delayed effect.'

Monsieur Crépeau blinked at the shocked faces around him.

'I don't understand,' he murmured, scratching his chin. 'I don't remember – ' Suddenly he yawned. His head lolled onto his neck; a moment later he was sound asleep.

(Clearly, being a pigeon must have been very tiring.)

Everyone stared at the snoring Monsieur Crépeau in silence. Professor Rathbone cleared his throat and glared at Ernie.

'I'm waiting, Ernie. **Who** are these people and what are they doing in my Weather Simulation Room?' He looked up at 2.0. 'And why is your robot so **BIG?**'

Ernie glanced at me for a long moment and I knew that he was going to tell his uncle **EVERYTHING**. Quickly, I whizzed through my list of Reasonable Excuses for Ultimate Disasters. Unfortunately, there was *nothing* that seemed suitable for this *particular* situation.

Ernie shrugged. 'It's all **my fault, Uncle Rathbone,**' he said, not meeting my eye.

I blinked, absolutely certain I hadn't heard correctly.

'They were here for the tour. I – uh – I wanted to show them the Weather Simulation Room myself.'

Professor Rathbone listened in silence, his fingers furiously twisting the end of his beard.

'And I took them to see the Big-o-Meter. 2.0 got bigged by accident.'

I glanced at Broccoli who looked as confused as me. Instead of getting us in trouble, Rat-Bone was **protecting us.**

Ernie hung his head. 'I never meant for any of this to happen, Uncle Rathbone. I'm sorry.'

'Sorry?' echoed his uncle, who was now twisting his beard so fast I was sure he was about to pull it off. 'This was going to be the

BIGGEST

scientific breakthrough

of the

CENTURY.

And now it's destroyed!'

'It was an accident,' said Ernie quietly.

'Accident? **Real inventors** don't have accidents.'

I snorted. Ernie's uncle might have been a **genius**, but he'd clearly forgotten some of the BASICS of inventing. 'Actually, some of the best inventions in this world were created by *mistake*,' I said. 'There's a list in the *Inventor's Handbook*. You should read it.'

The professor's eye twitched. 'Excuse me?'

'And none of this is Ernie's fault. It's yours. This Weather Simulation Room was full of **design faults.** In fact, you should be *grateful* we turned up. We **stopped** a weathernova from getting out.'

The professor flushed. 'What are you talking about? This room was functioning perf—'

'Was it?' I interrupted, giving him an ESHA LASER GLARE. 'Because I'm sure there was a problem with the wind generator.'

The professor's mouth opened and shut. 'We fixed that,' he said hoarsely. 'How did—'

'As for Ernie, he's one of the BEST inventors I've ever met,' I continued, ignoring him. 'Not as good as me, of course, but you should really think about working with him. If there's one thing I've learnt about inventing—'

'Did you really stop a weathernova from getting out?' interrupted Professor Rathbone, looking at Ernie.

Ernie hesitated, looked at me, and then he nodded. The professor shut his eyes, took a deep breath and opened them again. 'Right. I want you out of my laboratory. All of you,' he said, glaring at us. He glanced at Monsieur Crépeau. 'Him too. As for you, Ernie, you'll be responsible for cleaning this entire room.' He glanced at 2.0 and shook his head. 'You and your robot. After you've told me about this weathernova.'

With a final tug of his beard, he turned back and stomped through the snow.

More cameras flashed. 'Professor! Professor! Is there anything you would like to—'

'GET OUT OF MY WAY!' he growled, pushing past the TV crew.

Ernie cleared his throat. 'Well – uh – thank you.'

I raised my eyebrows. 'Did you just thank me, Rat-Bone?'

His eyes NARROWED into slits. 'For nothing.' He pointed a finger at us. 'Don't think this changes anything between us, worms.'

'Wouldn't dream of it, AIR-BRAIN,' I retorted.

'I only saved *you* because *you* saved me. Now we're even.' He straightened his glasses and strode off. 'Come on, 2.0. We still need to polish you up before tomorrow if we're going to win the Brain Trophy.'

'Affirmative, Master Rathbone.'

'And call me Ernie. We're a team, you know.'

The cameras flashed as Ernie strode after his uncle, 2.0 clanking behind him.

'Well, that turned out better than I expected,' said Broccoli with a sniff.

Berty licked his face again. Broccoli giggled and scratched the top of his head. 'I'm sorry about what I said, Berty. If it wasn't for you and your Pooper Scooper, we wouldn't have been able to stop that weathernova.'

Berty dived into the snow, then popped out again, a teensy-tiny mound of powder wobbling on his head.

Archibald made a noise that sounded like, 'can we take him back already?'.

Monsieur Crépeau snored loudly. z z z

'Do you think he'll remember anything?' said Broccoli.

I shrugged. 'Hopefully not. Even if he does, I don't think he'll believe it. Adults never do.' I grinned. 'Besides, I think he'll be more worried about his TV appearance.'

'We'll be on there too,' said Broccoli, eyeing the cameras warily. 'Nishi's going to find out.'

I sighed. 'Probably. But even my DRONG of a sister can't be as bad as a SUPER-SWALLOWER WEATHERNOVA. And I can still get her something from the gift shop.'

'What about the contest?'

'What about it?'

'It's **tomorrow**. We need to think about what we're going to enter.'

I blinked in surprise. **'We?** I thought you quit.'

'Well, I un-quit. It's clear that you need my help. Our help, in fact,' he said, stroking a grumpy Archibald. 'Now that we've lost the RoarEasy, we're going to have to come up with something else. Unless you want to do it on your own?'

'No,' I said quickly, a bubble of warmth rising inside me. We might not have the RoarEasy any more, but I was absolutely certain that Broccoli and I could still win the Brain Trophy.

Together.

'And – I – uh – I'm sorry too. About before.' I stood up and held my hand out to him. 'Welcome back, James Bertha Darwin. Tortoise owner. Spi-droid hacker. Teacher rescuer.'

He grinned and shook my hand. 'So – any ideas?'

'**Always.** But we need to get Archibald ready for his inspection first. Just look at him. He clearly needs a makeover. In fact, I have a **genius** idea about how we can make his shell super shiny.'

Archibald glared at me.

'Esha, I don't think—' began Broccoli.

'He'll be the best-looking tortoise they've ever seen.
You'll see, Broccoli. We're going to pass this inspection and
win the Brain Trophy. How hard can it—'

'ESHA VERMA!'

In the doorway, looking absolutely *more WILD*
than a WEATHERNOVA, was my DRONG of a sister. Beside
her, with a **very cross** expression on her face, was Mum.

'ESHA, YOU'RE IN SO MUCH TROUBLE!'

' . . . be?'

THE END (for now . . .)

TORTOISE WELFARE
SOCIETY

CERTIFICATE
OF ACHIEVEMENT

This is to certify that

Archibald, son of Archimedes,

PASSED

his tortoise inspection with flying colours.

Shelbus Sheldon

Date: 15th June

President of the Tortoise Welfare Society

(T.W.S.)

Shell-o Pa,

I trust you are having an exciting adventure in the Gobi Desert. Your pictures looked most thrilling. You will, I am sure, have received news that I passed the tortoise inspection. I am, after all, an exemplary tortoise.

In other more exciting news, myself and the HUMANS had the pleasure of being shrunk. Like Great Grand-Pa Archipopolo, I am sure I could have made history with my diminutive dimensions. Unfortunately, the DRIPPY-HUMAN-PET and the ANNOYING-SHE-HUMAN returned us to our normal size before my adventures could even begin.

Baby T also continues to be a nuisance. I have never met an animal that can eat quite as much as him. Despite all my attempts, he has still not picked up Tortoish. I am starting to question if our species are, indeed, related. I am quite sure it is impossible.

Hope to see you soon,

 Archibald

P.S. The ANNOYING-SHE-HUMAN appears to be in trouble with the MA-AND-PA-HUMANS. I am not quite sure what the consequences of this will be yet. I will write again as soon as I know.

Design your own Laboratory Rooms

Thought you'd reached the end of ~~my~~ our second story?
Of course not!

I, Esha Verma, and my apprentice, Broccoli, challenge
you to design **three** rooms that you think should be
included in the Central Research Laboratory.

For each room, include its name, a short
description of what is inside it/what it does
and draw a picture of it.

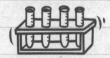

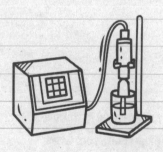

Name of the room: . . . .

Description: . . . .
. . . .

Name of the room: . . . .

Description: . . . .

. . . .

Name of the room: . . . .

Description: . . . .

. . . .

The Task of Ten

Fancy yourself an inventor? Here's your chance to prove it! Below I have given you a list of **ten items** that were in my Inventor's Kit during this adventure (until they fell out). See if you can use all ten to create your very own BRILLIANT invention:

(1) A pencil sharpener

(2) Two juggling balls

(3) A packet of tissues

(4) A twisted pan handle

(5) Five seashells

(6) Two pairs of rainbow shoelaces

(7) A roll of foil

(8) Cotton buds

(9) A ball of rubber bands

(10) One magnifying glass

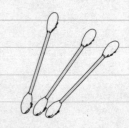

Draw here:

Name of invention: ....
. . . .

Build your own spi-droid spider

(trialled and tested by Ernie Rathbone)

Dear Reader,

Esha does not know that I have slipped this page into her journal (yet). Alas, I cannot tell you my TOP-SECRET instructions about building a spi-droid, but I can tell you how to create your own SPIDERS.

Uses: for scaring other inventors

What you'll need: pipe cleaners (any colour), googly eyes (the bigger and googlier the better), glue, pompoms (any colour), paper, scissors, card

1. Arrange four pipe cleaners horizontally in a line, one below the other.
2. Use your fingers to pinch all the pipe cleaners in the middle. Twist them a few times at this centre point until they are held together.
3. Wrap another pipe cleaner tightly around the centre point. This will form the base for you to stick your spider's head.

④ Stretch, bend and spread out the pipe cleaners sticking out from the centre point to create eight legs for your spider.

⑤ Fix a pompom to the pipe cleaner around the centre point using a small amount of glue. This will be your spider's head!

⑥ Once the glue has dried, you can add the googly eyes. Put a little glue on the back of each one and stick them to the spider's head.

Handy Tip: Use as many googly eyes as you want! You might find it easier to stick the googly eyes onto the pompom first and then stick the pompom onto the centre point once they have dried.

⑦ You can also cut out small triangles from paper or card to create mini pincers or teeth. Use a small amount of glue to stick these to your pompom head.

⑧ When the glue has dried, your spider is ready.

⑨ Repeat to make lots more spiders.

⑩ You are now ready to SCARE! Slip a spider or two into the bag of your ARCH-NEMESIS to give them an extra fright. Or you can keep them in your own to stop them NOSING around.

Build your own MINI Weathernova

(trialled and tested by Esha and Broccoli)

Uses: for learning more about weathernovas

What you'll need: funnel, an empty glass bottle and lid, glitter, water

1. Fill an empty glass bottle with water until it is roughly three-quarters full.
2. Use a funnel to pour some glitter into the bottle. The glitter will help you see your weathernova!
3. Seal the bottle.
4. Turn the bottle upside-down then move it AROUND and AROUND at LIGHTNING-FAST speed for a few seconds.
5. Put the bottle back down (it should still be upside down). You should now be able to see a mini weathernova inside it.

Hint: You might need to repeat step 4 a couple of times before you can see the weathernova properly.

WARNING: Do not, under any circumstances, take the lid off the bottle after the weathernova has formed. This could release it INTO THE WORLD . . .

The Art of Being Compacted:
TOP 10 TIPS

If you, the Reader, should ever find yourself compacted
and shrunk down to the size of an ant, I've included a list
of **TOP TIPS** to help you get around safely:

(1) When you are first compacted, everything else will look
ENORMOUS. Do not panic. You will get used to it.

(2) Listen carefully. Even the slightest noise might be a
sign of someone approaching.

(3) If anyone does approach, you should take cover
immediately.

(4) Always keep an eye open for hiding places. Table legs
are surprisingly useful for this.

(5) Don't forget to look UP.

(6) Give yourself extra time to get to places.

(7) Do not hitch a lift on people. It is likely you will fall
off and get squashed to a pulp.

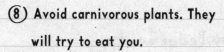

(8) Avoid carnivorous plants. They will try to eat you.

(9) So will animals.

(10) Carpets are **TROUBLE**. Stay away from them.

[A note from Broccoli: If you ask me, I would advise you not to get compacted in the first place.]

Acknowledgements

I'm extremely thankful to the following ULTRA-AWESOME people for helping me pull this book together.

Thank you to my wonderful agent, Lauren Gardner, for always believing.

A shout out to the BRILLIANT team at Macmillan for their support. Special thanks to my fantastic editor, Simran Kaur Sandhu, for our bonkers brainstorms and all the laughs.

Huge thanks to Allen, for his amazing illustrations, to Suzanne Cooper, Tracey Ridgewell and Sue Mason for their incredible design and to Amy Boxshall for her eagle eye.

Thanks to my LGS crew, for all their encouragement.

Finally, a MASSIVE thank you to my family, for sharing all my adventures.

About the Author

Pooja Puri is an ~~expert daydreamer~~ inventor of stories. Her debut novel *The Jungle* was published by Black & White's YA imprint, Ink Road, in 2017. *The Jungle* was subsequently nominated for the 2018 CILIP Carnegie Medal. *A Dinosaur Ate My Sister* is

her first middle-grade novel and the first book selected for the Marcus Rashford Book Club. *A Robot Squashed My Teacher* is the next in the series. She tweets @PoojaPuriWrites.

Here are 6 important things to know about her:

① She likes words.

② She also likes gumdrops (not expanding ones).

③ Her TOP 3 inventions are: the telephone, the ice-cream cone and glasses.

④ She once built a talking robot. It is now travelling somewhere in the Amazon.

⑤ She would like a pet dinosaur.

⑥ When Pooja is not inventing stories, she is working on a device that will let her talk to animals. It is not ready. Yet . . .

3 8002 02120 746 1